W9-BWS-003

A WOMAN IN THE SKY

Also published by Horizon Press

ANOTHER WORLD

James Hanley

A WOMAN IN THE SKY

HORIZON PRESS
NEW YORK

First published in the United States 1973
by Horizon Press

Printed in Great Britain
by Ebenezer Baylis and Son Ltd
The Trinity Press, Worcester, and London

Library of Congress Catalog Card No. 73-82070

ISBN 0-8180-0618 8

TO ARNOLD PALMER
(*in friendship*)

Two lonely elderly alcoholic women befriend each other.

I

'YES,' she said, 'yes.'

'And then?'

'She went on up.'

'Who went on up?' he asked, groping.

'Who'd you think?'

'That's what I'm asking you,' he said.

'Ask decent then, and keep your voice *down*,' Lil said.

'I presume you're referring to the unfortunate lady?'

'You presume correctly,' Lil replied.

'Ah!' he said, and 'Oh dear!'

'Here long?'

'Her? 'Bout three years, I think. Get them out of the way these days, push them up, under their feet, they say. How it is.'

'Oh!'

'Yes,' she said, 'yes.'

'Who are *they*?' he asked, magisterial in a moment.

'Who'd you think? Are you from that bloody council?'

'*No.*'

'Government then?'

'No!'

'Don't you shout at me,' Lil said.

'Not shouting, sorry, Mrs er . . . er.'

'The name is Winten,' Lil said, her voice sharpening. A smile broke, first of that evening.

'Sorry,' he said, 'you were saying . . .'

'Wasn't saying a thing.'

'What happened?'

'You know what happened. In the papers, walked out of the window.' He stood back, his mouth fell open, he stared.

'Walked . . . out of . . . the . . . window?'

'That's right.'

'But *why*?'

'Hasn't the answer now, has she? Well then.'

'I *am* sorry.' He saw her partly close her eyes, then peer at him. He felt awkward.

'Forgot,' she said, 'people do, you know, sometimes, just for a sec. Maybe she thought there was grass out there . . .'

'Grass?'

'What I said.'

'Who lives next door?'

'Us,' Lil replied.

'I mean on the other side,' he said, tentatively.

'Hargreaves lot. What about them?'

'Just wondered.'

'Fancy.'

'Hargreaves?' he said.

'That's right. Odd lot. I mean, well, take the mornings. First she goes on down, nobody knows where really, then she comes on back up, then he goes down, nobody knows where he goes neither, then he comes back up here. How it is.'

'How *what* is?' he asked, unable to disguise a sudden and pronounced irritability, but Mrs Winten appeared not to be listening.

'Strange about them Hargreaves lot.'

'Strange?'

'Said it. I mean the way he cared at first and she didn't, then after a while she was caring, and he wasn't, then both of them wasn't caring any more. How it is. Know what they said to him?'

'What?'

'Said he must, got to, had to, that's all. How it is.'

A new country, a new language, and he was uncertain of the soil, a foothold.

'Caring,' he said, again groping.

'About living *here*, of course, what else? Isn't terrace here, isn't brick, well is it?'

'Oh,' he said, 'I *see*,' not seeing. She lowered her eyes, refused to look at him, wondered when he would go.

'How long did you say the lady'd been here?'

'Three. Said it.'

He thought he heard her sucking her teeth, winced, finally stuttered, 'I see,' in the absence of anything else.

'Glad you do,' Lil said. 'Some people just don't!'

'How old was she?'

'Never asked,' and she clipped the words.

'Oh!'

'Can't even breathe round here now, leastways till they tell you to. Way it is.'

'Ahem! Um, yes . . . I understand,' he said.

'Glad you do.'

'Are the police upstairs?'

' 'Spect so.'

'I think I'll go up.'

'*Do* that then,' she said. He coughed again, muttered to himself, ahemmed.

'Did you know her very well?'

'Well as anybody knows anybody these days.' She suddenly brought up her apron as a shield, carefully watched him, and thought, 'people are terrible today, just terrible.' He jerked it out.

'Very sad.'

'Some things are,' and again she wondered when he would go.

'Can you tell me anything about Mrs Kavanagh?' he asked.

'Cried sometimes.'

'*Cried?*'

'That's right.'

'Awful,' he said, 'tragic,' then bumped his head against what was everywhere, concrete.

'Ow!'

'Ceilings are lowish, aren't they?'

'Something deeply wrong,' he thought.

'Something was wrong all along,' he said.

'Should've thought of that at the beginning,' and she wished he would go.

'I'll make further inquiries,' he said, the words dragging, and a sudden casualness evading her.

'If you want to do, *do*,' the words were bullets.

'Thank you.'

'Welcome.' He moved, she moved. He looked up, looked round, getting a feeling, looking for a meaning.

'Hardly call them halls,' he said, a ceiling beginning to press, turning to go, wanting to get out, into the air. He squeezed his way to the door, and his coat fell open.

'Oh dear,' she said.

'Anything wrong?'

'Nothing.'

'Goodbye, Mrs er . . . er,' he said, but she vanished when the door slammed. 'Extraordinary,' he thought, then went on up. Mrs Winten glimpsed her husband still sat in the dark corner.

'Who was that, Lil?' he cried.

'Collar back to front, Eddy.'

'Oh! They do come here sometimes, from some church, I think.'

'St Jude's.'

'That's it,' Eddy said, his knees hugged the electric fire. He lit his pipe, suddenly relaxed, spread legs, sent a cloud of smoke ceilingwards.

'What did *he* want?'

'About her, Eddy.'

'Oh! I see,' Eddy said, then mused.

'That's right. Poor thing. Lost she was, real lost. How it is, Eddy.'

'Ah! And how about it, Lil?' She got up and said nothing, and went off to the kitchen. Supper time, and all the suppers were cooking, up in the sky. She called.

'Fingers, Eddy?'

'Rightho,' he said, mused again. 'So someone actually called, did they? Well, well! Bastards,' a shout in his mind, sound of crashing glass.

'Coming!'

'Ta,' he shouted, then she came in with their supper. They sat.

'Eddy?'

'What?'

'Her friend went back in today.'

'Biddulph?'

'That's it.' Fork and finger dangled in air that was close, and the room bright.

'Drunk?'

'Lifting.' He grinned. 'Holloway again, 'spect.'

'She likes there best,' Lil said, even looked thoughtful about it. Eddy laughed, said he was glad somebody liked *something* and promptly swallowed a finger.

'Be public, Eddy,' she said, and she swallowed one, too.

'Pity she'd got nobody.'

'Had her, Mrs Biddulph, I mean. Great friends they were.'

'Aye.'

'News might have sent her through the window,' Lil said.

'Might.'

'Course, as I said to the chap with the collar, she might have lapsed, just for a sec maybe, thought she was flat, on the earth, I mean.'

'Could be,' and he swallowed another finger. 'How long d'you suppose her friend'll get?'

'Could be three this time. They don't like this lifting business at all.'

'Could be.'

'Poor dear. Happy as the day till they got her.'

'Sods.'

'Ah!' Lil said, 'ah!'

'Thinking about her just now, Lil,' Eddy said. 'Why only last Wednesday I bumped into her in The Marquis, gave her a Guinness.'

'Talked to her only yesterday,' Lil said.

'Once they get their orbs on you they never stop coming after you.'

'How it is.'

'Way she used to laugh, specially when she got her ration from the State.' First Lil smiled, then laughed. 'Of course. Can you hear her now?'

'Loved having the lucre Wednesdays, didn't she?'

'Loved blowing it,' Lil said.

'Only wanted to be left alone, but not everybody minds their own business.'

'Quite right, Lil. D'you know, I once saw two granite-faced bitches snooping round her old place, the place they pushed her out of, because they said they were going to knock it down, and then they didn't. Stupid bastards.'

'Where the grass used to be?'

'That's right,' Eddy said.

'God! The cod stuff they throw at you these days,' she said, 'all that stuff about making people happy. Ah! . . . she *was* happy.'

'Course she was. Remember saying to one of that probation lot, "Leave her *be*, she's all *right*, course she's drunk, and happy with it." But no . . . they wouldn't leave her be. Supposed to be a free country.'

'I remember that day, too. And she laughed, and they didn't.'

'Ah!'

'They love trying it on, don't they?'

'Telling me,' he said.

'Would've got her into the bin if they could.'

'Tried once, Friern Barnet or some such, wasn't it?'

'Think so.'

'Hope she's happy now, then.' Lil said nothing, feeling close to Mrs Kavanagh at that moment. Eddy laughed. 'That dream son of hers,' he said, 'that ship.'

'Codded them,' Lil said. She got up, wiped her mouth, went to the fire, sat, twiddled fingers. 'Electricity Board lot cut off her light only last Tuesday, Eddy.'

'Love obeying their own rules, Lil,' he said, at which she turned sharply, swung a hand tablewards.

'Shift that lot, Eddy.' Eddy did. He was like that. He liked doing things. He called in from the kitchen, 'shut that window, Lil,' and she got up, and shut it, there being a strong smell in the sky, Totall Point busy having its supper. He came in.

'Anything on the tele?'

'Dr Finlay.'

'Oh Christ! Not *again*?'

'Again,' she said, flat, then got up, began knob fiddling. First a scream, and then the picture.

'Football,' she said, 'oh no . . .!'

'Fine,' he said, sat down, lay back, watched the ball, listened to the screams.

She rested hands in an expansive lap, and closed her eyes, thinking again of one that had got lost, saw her, watched her go down into the world. Heard the Kavanagh feet, the cough, saw her very close, diminutive in a long black coat, and the big pockets, that were always empty, except on Wednesdays.

'Poor dear,' she said to herself, and then aloud, 'poor dear,' out of a slack mouth.

'What's that?' And Eddy came erect, but only a silence followed. Lil went on seeing her, hearing her steps, down and down, and up and up, and back again, the Kavanagh trudge. Every Wednesday. No change.

'You asleep there, Lil?' Her eyes were tight shut, she said nothing. 'Damn!' he shouted, the ball missing the net by inches. But she heard nothing, still Kavanagh close, spelling out days. Passing her inside window mornings, sometimes evenings, and there she was, stood in the other window, staring out at the sky that was always there. Rain Tuesday, and Kavanagh close to a fire, feeling cold. Saw her trotting off Wednesdays, her shining day of the week, listened to her shuffling steps, on a voyage by way of concrete mountains, avenues of silence, corridors of iron. Watched her pass under the blinking lights, moving towards a bigger light, like an eye over tall doors that were of steel. Saw the Kavanagh finger tentative on a red button, saw her pressing this, thus enabling a descent into caverns, and more lights blinking, and the patches of darkness that continued to yawn, wide and engulfing, and never hidden. Sometimes the corridors seemed longer, sometimes endless.

'Poor old dear,' and words falling into a silence.

'Half time,' Eddy said, but she said nothing.

'Lil!'

'What?' And her eyes closed.

'*Lil!*'

'*Well?*' and her eyes open.

'You falling asleep?'

'Thinking,' she said, again closed eyes.

'Oh!'

She snapped then. 'Oh *what?*'

'Nothing,' he said, closer to the screen now, and a referee in close-up. 'Thinking? What about?'

'Shut up.' Eddy shouted 'goal', but Lil had distanced again, thinking still about one that had got lost.

She wondered what he wanted, remembering the visitor, the tall man with the sandy hair, collar wrong way round.

'Must be from St Jude's,' she said. '*Must.*'

'What you muttering about now then?' he growled.

'Day before yesterday,' she said, mystery to Eddy, and he didn't pursue it, being lost in the crowd, swallowing the cheers.

'Damned football,' she said, but the cheering drowned her out. She leaned close, a hand on his shoulder, 'Eddy?'

'*Well?*' he snarled.

'You'll come to the funeral, Eddy, won't you?'

'Course I will. Buggers,' he said, 'buggers.'

'I wish . . .'

'Don't,' Eddy said, and jumped up crying, 'Bed.'

'Bed,' she said, throwing switches, following him to a room. An involuntary sigh escaped her, and she blurted out, 'Can't believe it still,' she said. Her sigh escaped him. He coughed loudly.

'Day's end,' he said, flopped into bed. She lay, was silent, still with closed eyes, and Eddy curled up beside her. Still Kavanagh close, remembering that all her days were perilous.

'Saw her going off only yesterday morning, saw her through her own window and her finger on a light switch, and very still she was, like she was uncertain about something. Dazed. Then she switched off and came out. See her now. Said good morning, and the tiniest smile at the corner of her mouth.' So Lil pondered, so the words dragged.

'Often saw her in The Marquis, stuck in the corner, sometimes Mrs Biddulph with her, recognize her laugh anytime. She'll miss her no end.' And now she watched her making the morning descent. 'Used to see her coming out of those dark lanes, sometimes she'd look back like she wasn't quite certain about something, couldn't make up her mind. Used to stop dead, too, look up at everything, fingers to her lips. I expect the whole lot of it bewildered her, really. Sheer size of the place. See her trotting to the lift. I once saw her standing so still I thought she was listening to the silence. Ah! I once watched her watch, from a dark corner. Strange then, strange.'

There was no voice and no movement. There were no railings and there was no park. There were no footsteps, and there were no people. And there was no grass. There was nothing.

'Nothing,' Lil said, loudly, abruptly, 'noth . . .'

'What you ah-ing about now?' Eddy shouted, then he turned over, curled up like a squirrel.

'Go to sleep, Eddy,' she said. Her voice seemed strangely distant, as though she were speaking to him from the end of their corridor.

'Know you're upset. Never harmed anybody. Sods.' And she said quietly, 'I'll slip along and see Biddulph, Friday.'

'*Do* that,' and again he turned over, wondered when Lil would give up, relax, lie still, *sleep*. 'Try and settle, can't you?' he said. Her voice dropped, and then she felt a sudden pressure upon her own eyelids.

'Still can't believe somehow . . .'

‘Enough is a bloody *’nough. Go* to sleep.’

‘All right, Eddy, I will.’

‘Thank God for that,’ Eddy said, and again the words that she could not hold.

‘Kind of queer, the whole thing, too sudden.’

‘There are some things that are queer. All right?’ Then flung another word very close to her ear. ‘*Please*!’ But she had already gone, back into yesterday, a closeness gone, Eddy gone, remembering only a fleeting moment and a smile, and later the other sounds that she did not like.

‘That glass,’ she cried, ‘Oh God! Eddy.’ So she was back at the beginning. No sound and no footstep, and no echo. Only the silence, and the lifts dead. Eddy snored.

*

Opening her eyes into the darkness, she suddenly saw the helmet and the buttons. These shone. And Lil listened.

‘What happened, madam?’ the helmet said.

‘She went out, fell,’ Lil said.

‘We *know* that.’

‘*Well?*’

‘Well what?’

‘Nothing. Nothing at all. Go away.’

‘Who *are* you?’

‘Who’d you think?’ asked Lil.

‘Not thinking. Just asking, madam,’ the helmet replied.

‘Ask civil then.’

‘I *am*.’ His boots squeaked, she saw him begin rocking on his heels.

‘Well then?’

‘Tell me about her,’ said the helmet, and she told.

‘Five foot three, and lived in a big overcoat,’ Lil said. ‘Never looked up much, went about the world like a mouse, quiet like, said nothing, lived in corners, asked nothing, went her way, then came back from wherever she went to, her business only. Saw her yesterday, said "hello". Hated the wind, hated the lifts going dead, upset her no end, saw her cry once. Used to plug her ears when it blew, lie on the kitchen floor, talked to herself aloud, against the noise, even heard her once, place used to rock betimes, I mean rocked, hated where she was, knew it from the beginning . . .'

'Continue, madam.'

'Sometimes she used to walk so slowly you'd think that one foot was playing truant on the other,' Lil said. 'Had one friend!'

'Name?'

'Biddulph.'

'Address?'

'Don't know.' He rocked again, the squeaks rose, he cleared his throat, was then solemn.

'Lots of things you don't appear to know, madam,' he said. 'Happen to know where she is *now*?'

'No,' Lil said, then very pronouncedly, 'and there are some things you don't want to know.' When he leaned in, Lil leaned back.

'What d'you suppose made her jump clean through a window miles high?'

'Yesterday she . . .' faltered, 'I mean . . .'

'*What* do you mean?'

'She was heavy with something when she come back yesterday,' Lil said. 'Saw it, felt it.'

'Heavy with what, and what, by the way, is *your* name?'

'Winten. Anything else?'

'Right. Heavy with *what*?'

'Don't know. Sad, I expect.' Still rocking, still casual, the helmet said, 'And why would you suppose the lady was sad, madam?'

'Heard they wouldn't have her back, I believe,' replied Lil.

'Who heard they wouldn't have her back, and who's they, and where's where?'

'Holloway, I believe.'

'Like that is it?'

'Like that it is.'

'I *see*.'

'Glad you do.'

'She was up before that lot only yesterday,' Lil said, 'but the chap up front of her told her to go, wouldn't let her go back in because she wanted to.'

'*What* chap?' And Lil for the first time screeched, 'Find *out*.'

'Where were you when she threw herself out? And even that's a bit dicey, missus, you just can't jump *through* them.' He seemed to wait an age for the answer.

'Climbed up, I expect. What else?'

'Ahem. Um! Well now, where were you at the time?' And Lil snapped back, 'Minding my own business.'

'*Where*?'

'In . . . my . . . *kitchen*,' and after a pause the louder shout, 'that enough?'

'You *are* jumpy,' the helmet said, stopped rocking.

'Anything else?' she asked.

'May I come in?'

'You mayn't.'

'What did you do when you heard the crash?'

'What d'you think? Went on down. Found her. Picked her up, and then I put her down again, quickly.'

'Thank you,' he said. 'And you don't know anything about her friend, or where I can find her. It *is* serious, madam.'

'No, I don't.'

'You will be called as a witness.'

'Call me.' He turned as if to go, then turned again, studied her.

'So she was Old Street way yesterday, was she? What for, d'you expect?'

'Find out. May I close my door . . . *sir*?'

'Nobody stopping you, madam,' he said, suddenly put a foot on the step, leaned close. 'You can close it now, but you'll have to open it again tomorrow, won't you,' and he smiled in her face.

'What for?'

'Witness to the *fact*, lady.' She drew back, rattled the knob, and he said, 'That's all.'

'Well then?'

'Nothing. And thank you for the information, madam. We'll check up on the lady you mentioned. What was her name again?'

And Lil shouted in his face, '*Biddulph*.'

'No need to shout. No need to lose your temper.'

She watched him go, heard his heavy steps, echoing as he distanced. She banged the door, wondered if a day had ended.

'Eddy!' He woke, sat up in the darkness. 'What the *hell*?' Eddy rubbed his eyes, groped for the switch, flooded the room, and then he saw her, sat up, stiff, and staring, staring.

'God, missus, you are upset,' hugging her. 'I'll get you something, Lil,' and she went on staring, and didn't mind what Eddy got, she was so glad of the light, and Eddy *there*, after the darkness, after the walk through yesterday.

'Here,' and the glass at her lips, 'drink it, but first drop these pills down, make you sleep, it'll be tomorrow when you wake up, and you'll be all right then, Lil, you will, really. It's that bloody noise and going down and finding her, ah, come on now, drink it.'

'Where'd you get it, Eddy?'

'What the *hell* does that matter?' and she drank, felt his arms around her, and was glad of that, the arms' warmth.

'Eddy?'

'What?'

'Oh . . . nothing . . . just glad,' and he hugged her tighter, loving her, being sorry.

'There now,' he said, as mother to child. 'Lie down. Had a bad dream, that's all. Those pills'll put you asleep in no time,' and she lay back, and he with her.

'Sorry I woke you.'

'Ah!' He plunged the room into darkness. 'Fall asleep,' he said, knowing she was glad he was there, with the arm's warmth. He patted her, then turned away and lay flat on his back, hands behind head, the eyes closed, and he, too, remembering.

'Horrible shock for Lil.' He turned over again, buried his head in the pillows, listened, waited, noting her heavy breathing.

'You all right?'

Lil slept. Later, he snored.

*

The Kavanagh world was closed for the night, the bed empty, and the room soundless. And here in the room were 'her things'. But daylight's eyes would narrow when the world opened again, and a first glint of light would come through a high window, that was yet wide to the sky. It would touch table, bed, and chair, and as the light grew it would grope further and further into the silence, finding a chair on its back under the window, and on the table a small cardboard box containing the dream letters that had never been posted. The cupboard would yawn with its own emptiness, and the Electricity Board could shut off the light forever. Echoes of past journeys would recede into distances. The shared world of corners, and shadows and silence with one that had also gone, and now crouched in a place where the smells were sometimes high and sometimes low, and always the same smells: carbolic, Lioness powder, pee. She would think of a meeting that had died, and the words after it. She, too, remembered yesterday, and another place, and the chill of it as she stood for a fugitive moment or two, after which she had hurried out, there no longer being reason in it. A ritual of days broken, and the journeys that were always the same journeys, ended. One upright, and one bent, one tall and one small, and the names of their days engraved with the meanings that were in them. Mondays to the park, to sit and watch others go by, and Tuesdays to the library where it was always warm, and this free. Peaceful, strangely silent, gently snoring away time at a table piled with the books that they did not read, the one leaning to the other in a forest of bent heads. And Wednesdays to the Post Office, and the man that would smile at them, as he watched one write 'Brigid' with a drunken hand, and the other mark with an X as big as herself, so the State knew that somebody was still around. After which the notes crackled and the two women would smile at each other, and shuffle out, and a bell strident onto the silent street. And arm in arm, and a little bent, and the feet moving off in the only direction, the shortest journey to the place where the lights shone, and the glasses tinkled, the orchestra of voices never changing tempo, and none would cry for coda. Nobody noticed them, and nobody spoke to them, yesterday's fragments. Even their language seemed strange, and it contained no key. The only one lay in a faraway office, and it did not matter now. This office was small, and was rendered smaller by a too large desk, at which a man and a woman sat. The man was bent over a ledger, and his pencil slowly erased a name from the book. The woman assembled, and then disassembled several pieces of paper, finally laid them down and looked across at the man opposite her.

'I'll look her up this afternoon,' Mrs Laurent said. The man, Jenkins by name, said quietly, 'Yes, do that.'

'Quite frankly I don't know what to do with Biddulph now,' she said.

'It's a business, isn't it?' His words razor sharp, and then he sat back, contemplated the woman. 'Always admired your patience.' There were other things he admired about her, too, but she made no responses.

'What'll you do with the stuff?'

'Get rid of it.'

'Of course.'

'Strange that you couldn't find a single relative of any kind.'

'Nothing is strange,' she said, again fidgeted with her papers. 'That woman is the most independent creature I've ever come across. She may not accept what's offered.'

'Her business,' he said, took out a cigarette, lit it, sent smoke flying everywhere.

'She'll have to be pushed,' Mrs Laurent said.

'She has a family.'

'She's not wanted. Told me that. Left that lot long ago.'

'People are just queer,' Jenkins said, and Mrs Laurent looked at him as though he had not spoken a word.

'Time?' she asked. A glance at his wrist. 'Just five past,' he said.

'Good.'

'I once asked Biddulph how she and Kavanagh first met.'

'And then?'

'Picked her out of the gutter one midnight. Quite prone. Took her home. They seemed glued to each other after that. Apparently Kavanagh told her that she first got really blind when she was only fifteen and a half . . .'

'Good God!'

'They both of them worked in the same big house at one

time, somewhere in the Maida Vale area. They were both sacked, they couldn't be parted from the bottle.' She paused suddenly, and then Jenkins watched her smile, then laugh.

'I once asked Mrs Kavanagh what she liked best of all, and she said, sitting down at the end of the day, I mean after the others were satisfied.' Jenkins smiled, too. 'Duty done,' he said, sent another violent cloud upwards. 'Oh! By the way, Mrs Laurent, same place this evening?'

'As you wish.' Christian names were yet very private territory in the little room with the giant desk.

'I'm taking Biddulph to the funeral,' she said, gathered her papers together, and got up. He watched her pack her briefcase.

'Rightie-ho,' he said.

'Around five then,' she said, picked up the briefcase and left, not forgetting to send echoes down the corridor from a loudly closed door. He idled with the pages of a book, sent them flying backwards and forwards, with an occasional pointless glance at the clock that had died forty-eight hours previously.

*

Mrs Laurent meanwhile sped to her car, to her purpose and duty. She had not been expected, and little knew as she passed into the gaunt building that she was not wanted. But she came, since this was the thing to do. Mrs Biddulph was much alone in a rather crowded room.

'Well now! And how are we today?' The woman addressed made no reply, and did not look up. She just *felt* the visitor there.

'Well now,' she repeated, and caught the Biddulph arm, prised her free, and moved to the door, and waited for this to open. Mrs Biddulph stood quite still, refused to look up, and did not speak. The door opened and they went into another room, where in a far corner a watcher watched, and uttered the single word, 'yes'.

'Come along now,' Mrs Laurent said, and at last the woman looked up at her visitor. Yes, it *was* her. How often they had been close together, and how well they knew each other. Mrs Biddulph was sometimes critical, and was so now.

'Why'd you wear such ridiculous floppy hats?' she asked. 'Bloody silly you look,' but her visitor led her away quietly to a small table, made her sit down, and then followed suit. This room, too, was filling up, the world creeping in, for the usually allotted time.

'That's right,' and the visitor put down her briefcase. The woman opposite then barked out, 'What d'you want *now*?' Another Laurentian smile. 'I like my floppy hats, Mrs Biddulph.'

'Still look bloody silly to me.'

'I asked you how you were,' the eye steady, the tone of voice severe.

'How'd you think I am?'

'I'm asking you. I understand you had a visit from Mrs Kavanagh's neighbour. Nice of her to call.'

'Never asked her,' Mrs Biddulph said.

'That's what makes it nice,' said the visitor. The Biddulph hands were tight at the table edge, then suddenly clenched, and drawn inwards. She then leaned back in the chair, surveyed the visitor.

'That's better.'

'Won't get me with softness,' Mrs Biddulph said.

'If she hadn't called you'd have had nobody,' Mrs Laurent said.

'You *know* that, dear.'

'Don't know anything.'

'You know what they'll do, too.'

'Don't care what, really.'

'Mr Jenkins asked after you.'

'What for?'

Mrs Laurent leaned across, smiled. 'Because he's a nice man.'

'Save a lot of trouble if people were nice at the right time,' and the raised voice brought the watcher nearer, who, bending over Mrs Biddulph said quietly, 'watch it', and returned to her sentry post.

'What'll you do if you *get* out?'

'How'd I know *that*?'

'Keep your voice down, dear.'

'Ah! . . .' and the Biddulph eyes were once more downcast, and this time she absolutely refused to look up.

'Look at me.'

'What for?' And she felt a hand covering the clenched fists.

'I'm your friend,' Mrs Laurent said.

'Friend?' The laugh came short and sharp. '*Friend*?'

'I *know* you.'

'Sure you do. World's full of wonders.'

'Your own fault. Been warned time enough.'

'Always warning people, and don't you just love doing it.'

'It's about the flat,' Mrs Laurent said.

'*What* flat?'

'Your friend, Mrs Kavanagh's flat.'

'What about it?'

'She left things. They're yours.'

'Don't want them.'

'Don't be stupid.'

'*Keep* them.'

'You'll be glad of the money.'

'Ah! . . .'

'A new tenant coming in there, must get rid of the flat's

contents,' and, after a momentary pause, 'the council won't wait.'

'Why don't you just go away,' Mrs Biddulph said.

'The council would have let you have the flat yourself, I'm sure, considering the circumstances, but you've always hated the place.'

'Always did.'

'I said the money would come in handy. You *were*, I hope, listening.' Mrs Biddulph half rose, leaned across the table, and so close, that the visitor drew back.

'Would have been with us *now*,' snarled Mrs Biddulph, 'if you hadn't gone and told someone I'd been lifted.'

Mrs Laurent pushed the woman back into the chair.

'I don't lift anybody,' she said. 'I'm only concerned with them *after* they've been lifted, as you call it.'

'Sent her through the bloody window.'

Ignoring this the visitor again stressed a point. 'The money, the proceeds from Mrs Kavanagh's *things*. You'll be glad of it,' but there was no answer. 'And there are other things to be considered.' But the Biddulph head was still down and it refused to come up. The visitor decided to be patient. She knew her charge, understood her aggressiveness, a most positive militancy that never extended beyond the area that contained it.

'I've brought you something, dear,' Mrs Laurent said.

'What for?' The visitor smiled. 'Only a little cake,' she said.

'Keep it.' She noted another smile, and said, acidly, 'And there's no need to smile about it, neither.' But the smile held, a known way through particular country.

'You don't suppose I'd call without bringing you something.'

'I was just minding my own business,' Mrs Biddulph said, 'and now see what's happened. Why'd you go on lifting people when they're happy? And you can have that *straight*.' And Mrs Laurent at once accepted it, it being the thing to do. She bent down and took a small parcel from the briefcase, and put it on the table.

'There!'

'Keep it,' the voice raised, and the head up, which turned sharply to look at the clock, and to catch the eye of the watcher, watching.

'That lot hear every bloody word you say.'

'Don't you want it?'

'No.'

'We made every kind of inquiry, but without result.'

'Could've told you that. She only had me.'

'And the money?'

'I'll think about it.'

'You won't think about it at all. You'll say plain yes or no. If you don't want the things, they can go to Mrs Winten next door.'

'Why don't you leave me alone,' Mrs Biddulph said.

'All right. And we'll keep the money until you come out.'

'Haven't even been tried yet.'

The visitor's soft laugh came as a surprise of the day.

'You can't do anything with it, if you're *in*, can you?'

'God! You are sure, aren't you?' Mrs Biddulph leaned in again. 'I could have it in my hand, look at it, know it was mine. If I say one thing, you always say something else. Pops out of your head like magic. Know everything, don't you?'

'You've never been an easy customer,' Mrs Laurent said.

'Glad I haven't.' The visitor glanced at her watch, checked with the clock, caught the watcher's eye, and expected the usual at any moment now. So far everything had worked out according to rule. She had called once more to see a professional 'lifter', and the pattern never changed.

'I can *never* get near to this woman,' she thought. The

Laurent hand suddenly stroked the Biddulph fist. 'You know I'm sorry about this, Mrs Biddulph, you *do* know.'

'Fancy that.'

'Mrs Biddulph?'

'*Well?*'

'I've been handy for you many a time, and you know it.'

'D'you know what?'

'What?'

'I've never once been private in my whole life,' Mrs Biddulph said.

'You've travelled pretty well,' replied Mrs Laurent. 'I'll look in on you next week.' There was no reply. Heads turned the moment the clock struck.

'You wouldn't believe this, but I remember every single word you said to me,' but the visitor wasn't listening, and had turned her head away, received the expected nod from the end of the room, and rose to her feet.

'What's this?' The watcher bent over the table.

'Only a small cake,' Mrs Laurent said.

'Well, see about it.'

'Of course.' She stood watching Mrs Biddulph, hands deep in her pockets, depart with the others. She paused at the door, waited.

'Hello,' the watcher said.

'Hello.'

'Cheered some of them up, seeing her back, I mean,' the watcher said.

Mrs Laurent found a weary word, dragged the reply, 'Ye . . . s.'

'Can I get you a cup of tea?'

'No thanks. Somebody waiting for me outside.'

'Felt sorry for her this morning. *Cried.* First time I ever saw her do it.'

'They were devoted to each other,' said Mrs Laurent.

'You knew her quite well.'

'Of course.'

'Goodbye.'

'Goodbye.' Mrs Laurent came out into the corridor. 'She'll die here,' she thought, then, suddenly remembering that Jenkins would be waiting outside, increased her pace, and the moment she got through the gate she saw him, faithful unto death, Jenkins, who now hurried forward to meet her with a ready smile.

'How's the lame dog?'

'*Lame.*'

'Of course,' and he took her arm and hurried her across the road.

'I do admire your patience, Mrs Laurent,' Jenkins said.

They drove off, heading West.

*

All the doors in this building were closed, and one wasn't. Lil asked Eddy if he was coming in, or going out.

'I meant to . . . ah, doesn't matter now,' Eddy said, came in, shut the door.

'Say it,' she said.

'Thinking about Kent,' Eddy said, 'need a break after this lot.'

'I'll think about it.'

'Ta. Knew you would.' He watched her cut his sandwiches, walked round the table, held her.

'Lil!'

'There! That's done,' she said, and packed the sandwiches into the tin box.

He leaned to her, his voice trembled a little as he said, 'I'm just plain worried that you don't like it here any more, Lil.'

'And I'm sick of this kitchen,' she cried, and rushed away to the sitting room. She sat down, wondered when he would go. She wanted to be alone. The thought broke the moment he sat beside her.

'How'd you know I liked it anytime?' she asked.

'You never said, not once . . .'

'You never asked,' she said.

'It's our home, Lil.' Flustered, she said quickly, 'Everything's all so sudden, Eddy.'

'Ah!' Hugging her, he said, 'I'd hate you not to be happy, Lil,' and he was glad when she smiled.

'I'm all right. I'll think about Kent,' she said.

'I'm glad. Wish you hadn't promised to go *there*.'

'I promised,' Lil said, the words coming through her teeth. 'You *know* I did.'

'All right, all *right*.' She took his hand, pressed it. 'There are some things you just have to remember.'

'I know.'

'We're lucky, Eddy, and she wasn't.'

'Yes, yes, I know that,' and he could not disguise a sudden irritation.'

'She had nothing, and we have.'

'Know that, too.'

'I never wanted to come here, but I came. So did the others.'

'Better than nothing,' he said.

'Anything's better than nothing. You're always right, Eddy.'

'We got mixed up in this, it can't be helped, Lil.'

'Have to be sorry for people some time,' she said.

'Of course.'

'I got mixed up, too,' Lil said.

'I know,' automatically, like the parrot.

'I shall go on Friday, Eddy,' she said, 'and I'll go on the next Friday, too, if she asks me.'

'Then *go*.'

'I shall.'

'All *right*.'

'And there's no need to go worrying about me.' The grip on her hand tightened, and he said, almost shyly, 'Perhaps I do fuss a bit, Lil, but it's only because I love you. There!'

'You're a good man to me, Eddy,' Lil said.

A tension was dying down, the ice melting, the world that was pushing its nose in was having it pushed out again. Eddy felt relief. Clouded thoughts came clear. 'Wish it'd never happened,' he thought, 'wish she hadn't noticed, wish everything was just ordinary again.'

'I won't say another bloody word about it,' he said.

'I shouldn't.'

'I'll just slip out for the paper,' he said.

'Do that.' She folded hands in a lap, she gave a big sigh. 'Poor Eddy, wish he didn't fuss so much,' and suddenly longed for contentment. 'Funny, when I looked through the window this morning it was like I'd done it for the first time. Strange feeling, couldn't stop myself, had to, that's all.' She got up and walked slowly round the room, and then went on to the other two rooms, glanced in the bathroom, the kitchen, then returned and sat down on the couch.

'He's quite right, it is our home. Just being silly, that's what.'

The whole thing seemed like a study in still life. The heavy, ugly furniture froze where it stood, and the stiff curtains rarely moved. Most evenings she spent alone, the television set on, absorbing what came out of it. Not a speck of dust about. The whole room had the indestructible air of the day before yesterday.

'I wish he wasn't going out tonight,' she thought, and then Eddy returned with the evening paper.

'Must be off now,' he said.

'Yes, I know,' she said.

'Check the tele for you, Lil.'

'If you want to.'

'Course I *want* to.' But the set seemed miles away, and as she watched him checking through the channels she could only think of the woman she would visit again next Friday.

'Poor creature. And so lonely, I'm sure,' she thought.

'Good Old Days,' announced Eddy, and dropped the paper in her lap. 'It'll do.' The moments were suddenly pregnant with over emphasis.

'I'll try and see if I can get back earlier,' he said. 'And you *will* think about what I said, Lil. Kent, I mean.'

'I'll think about Kent.'

'I didn't want to go out tonight,' he said, 'not really.'

'That's not fussing,' Lil said, 'it's just stupid.'

'Suppose it is.'

Eddy dawdled, and she wanted to cry, 'get off', wanting to be alone, the tele on, getting lost again, being taken out of herself. She put a finger on the switch, then hesitated. She listened to echoing feet down the corridors, the loud slamming of doors, the world coming back in the evening, the lifts working overtime. She heard the bedroom door close, and suddenly he was there again, leaning over her, saying, 'Off now,' for the twentieth time. She followed him to the door.

'Bye.'

'Bye,' he said, gave her a quick peck, and shot through the door. She watched him stride into the darkness, then shut the door. She switched on, saw the figures on the screen, listened to the laughter, into which Eddy himself had suddenly vanished. She lay back on the couch, relaxed, forgot all about yesterday. But suddenly it had returned, unannounced, and when she heard the knock she got up and opened the door. A man in a black suit, raincoat over his shoulder, a dangling briefcase in his hand.

'Yes?'

'Mrs Winten?'

'Well?'

'Is she in?'

'I'm Mrs Winten. What d'you want?'

'Oh,' he said, and then, 'Ah! . . . I . . .'

'Who are you?'

'Council,' he said. 'Mr Thompson.'

'Oh yes.'

'It's about the flat next door.'

'What about it?'

'We want to clear it.'

'Clear it?'

'That's right,' Mr Thompson said.

'*What* a time to call about that,' she said.

'Sorry. Duty calls, madam. You don't understand, I'm sorry,' and he put a foot on the step.

'I don't.'

'Can I come in for a moment.'

'No. You can't,' Lil said.

'Oh.'

'Say what you want, and be done with it.'

'You were the deceased's nearest neighbour?'

'That's all over.'

'Not quite,' he said. 'I'm looking for a friend with whom she used to live,' and the notebook came out, the pencil poised, 'Yes?'

'You'll have to go to Holloway,' Lil said. 'She's on remand there.'

'I *see*.'

'That all?'

'We want to clear the flat for the new tenant coming in,' he said.

'They are in a hurry,' Lil said, and it drew the first Thompsonian smile.

'Nobody likes to be kept waiting these days, madam.'

'That's where she is then.'

'Her name, please?'

'Biddulph. Mrs Lena Biddulph.'

He patted his briefcase. 'We have the particulars here,' he said.

'Then why bother me?'

'Did you know the deceased well?'

'Just neighbours.'

'There appears to be no existing relative,' he said.

'Mrs Laurent knows all about that.'

'Laurent?'

'Probation.'

'Oh! I see. Thank you. Sorry to have bothered you, madam.'

'Quite all right,' she said, and he saw her hand reach for the door knob.

'You're quite high up here,' he said, turned to go, offered her a wintry smile. 'You've a spare key, no doubt?'

'I have.'

He held out his hand. 'Thank you, Mrs Winten. I'll just take a look round. A regrettable business,' and when she moved, he moved, put on his hat, and went off to the empty flat.

'Well!' she exclaimed, 'at this time of the day.' She heard the door open and close again, went out, and stood looking through the window. She saw the torch, the man moving about the room, and then he switched on the light.

'Never cut it off after all,' and she slipped back, and waited by the open door. She did not have long to wait.'

'Thank you. I'll retain the key. Good evening.'

'Good evening,' and then he was gone. His footsteps died away, she closed the door, sat down. The noise was still there, the voices in the room. She got up and switched off the set. 'Looked so cold, so empty,' she thought, seeing the man again, the dark room and the flashing torch. She made herself comfortable again, closed her eyes, and thought about Eddy. Unusual for him he had dropped in at The Grapes and got himself a whisky, gulped it down, and rushed off again. Along the same road, a turn into the same street, round the same corners, no change in the set rhythm of his day. The traffic lights blinked at him, the same people passed him by, and a newsvendor called out, 'Hello, Ed.' He was glad of these simple things, and they were important to him. He caught the same bus, and alighted at the same stop. But his eye was yet full of the room, and the woman in it. He hoped she'd enjoy 'Good Old Days'. Pity she was out mornings, and he nights. Their worlds would always tug against each other. He hoped she would think about Kent, she worried him, she hadn't got over that terrible shock, a change would do her good. Never seen her so upset. Once, he felt he was talking to a quite different person altogether. Everything seemed so simple, so certain, and then . . .

'Sorry, mate,' he called to the man that had bumped into him, but the man only scowled and said nothing. It was with a sense of relief that he saw the market ahead of him. *His* world. The same as yesterday, and the same tomorrow. He stopped dead in his tracks, the big gate suddenly yawning at him. 'Here we are.'

He could not understand why at this moment the two old women came into his mind. 'Ah! Fancy having *nobody*,' he thought. The faces appeared to be staring down at him, but he saw only Lil, sitting in front of the television set, the door closed, and the room warm. 'Glad when it's all over.' He had a last glimpse of Lil as he passed through the gate. And Lil was real.

II

YESTERDAY.

'This way, madam,' the man said, alert, eager, thrusting himself into the new day. '*This* way.' She stood, irresolute, heard echoing footsteps in a long corridor, heard a clock tick loudly.

'Which way?' she said.

'There's only *one* way here, madam,' the man said, the words incisive in her ear, and he walked on, and she followed, drowned in her overcoat. She made an abrupt halt.

'Are . . . *you* . . . *coming*?'

'Yes, yes . . .'

'Then come,' and the echoes convoluted, up and down.

'Where *are* you, madam?'

'Here.'

'Then do come along,' the man said, leaned closer to her ear. 'The world is very busy this morning, in spite of your refusal to accept the fact.'

'What's that?'

'Nothing,' the echo following.

'I see.'

'You *don't* see.'

'I think I do,' she replied.

'*Do* you now?'

'Where are we going?'

'Same place as last time, madam, and I did tell you, well,

didn't I? There's only one way here.' And they went on, she trailing. He turned suddenly. 'Did I hear you say something?'

'Wasn't saying a word,' the woman replied. 'I was just thinking.'

'Could be painful. You're always thinking, why don't you stop thinking, once in a while?' He lined the words with acid.

'I'm not quite myself this morning, sir,' she said.

'You said that the last time.'

'Saying it this time,' she said. He halted, turned, faced her. 'You just can't help it, can you, madam?'

'What's that?' groping again. And he said, '*nothing*.' A thin smile followed, and he added, 'Can you recall the last time you were here?'

'What's that? Sorry.' He spelt it in her right ear. 'D'you remember the last occ*as*ion?'

'I'm not quite myself this morning,' the woman said.

'You told me that already.' She stopped again.

'What *now*? Anything wrong?'

'Is there? I don't know.' And then he was closer still. 'What do you know? You're as familiar to me as the hairs on my chest, madam.'

'Thank you.' And he thought, 'What on earth is she thanking me for?'

'Do hurry, madam, the gentlemen are waiting.'

'Oh God!' she said, out of a dry throat.

'What's that you said?' And the leaden word rolled the length of the corridor.

'Nothing.' He took her arm. 'Where did they find you *this* time?'

'What's that?'

'Never said a word, madam. *This* way.'

'Oh yes.' And when she heard the stentorian voice cry

out, she knew she was back again, in known country. Yet another clock ticked, and the murmurs were waves.

'Brigid Kavanagh!' And the man beside her hissed in her ear, 'There. That way. Over *there*, madam. That's right.'

'Thank you.' But he had gone, and he had said nothing, so she cried out, 'Here,' and then she entered and another door closed behind her.

'Brigid Kavanagh?' and the voice nearer.

'Yes, sir.' The clerk leaned close, whispered. '*Again*, your worship.'

'I can see that. To some things there seems no end.'

'No, your worship.' Mr Faulkner boomed. 'Your face, madam, is becoming too familiar here.'

'What's that, sir?' An usher ushered, towered. 'Take the book in your right hand.'

'Which hand?'

'*Your* . . .'

After which she sensed, and said, 'right hand.'

There was a momentary silence.

'Brigid Kavanagh!'

'Yes, your honour.'

'You're here again.'

'Yes, sir.'

'You were here a week ago, and were let off with a caution.'

'Yes, sir,' she replied, and for a moment thought the gentleman was actually smiling at her.

'You would appear to like the atmosphere here,' Mr Faulkner said. The titters flew like sparrows.

'*Silence*!' She had lowered her head, tightly gripped her hands.

'Quiet please.' Mr Faulkner leaned violently to his left. 'What, *this* time?'

'Drunk, and making a nuisance.'

'I see. Proceed.' He closed his eyes, listened for the grey monotones, got them.

'At half past three yesterday afternoon I found the accused sitting on a bench at the bus stop.' Pause.

'Continue please.' She droned. 'She was drunk, and singing. A small crowd had gathered. She was shaking hands with everybody. One gentleman missed his bus because she would not leave go of his hand . . .'

'Oh!'

'I then arrested her, your worship.'

'Thank you,' Mr Faulkner said, again conferred with his clerk.

'Is Mrs Laurent here?'

'Over there, your worship.' Mr Faulkner dropped his voice, 'I think I'll adjourn this case,' and then sat up. '*Mrs* Kavanagh?'

'Yes, sir.'

'How old are you?'

'Sixty.' And the clerk whispered, 'Seventy-six, your worship.'

'Where do you live?'

'In the sky,' and a lone titter following.

'*Silence.*'

'Where do you *live*?' Mr Faulkner preferred the conspiratorial whispers of his clerk.

'New tower block, Mr Faulkner. Totall Point.' He paused a moment, and then added, 'Known as Total Extinction, your worship.'

'Indeed! That the best they could do?' He faced the clerk directly, who hadn't got the answer.

'Where is this building, madam?'

'Near the darkness.' And he thought, 'Poor dear. Hasn't even connected yet.'

'Have you any children?'

'One son, sir.'

'His name?'

'Sean Kavanagh, your worship.'

'Where is he now?'

'On a ship.'

The clerk's words were soft against the Faulkner ear: 'There is no ship.' Ignoring this, Mr Faulkner put the question.

'Tell me about your son,' he said. The world waited.

'Tell the magistrate about your *son*, madam, and the name of his *ship*.'

'*Devonian*, sir.' The clerk, Beech by name, leaned closer still.

'She has no son, your worship. There is no ship. There never was. I *know*.' Mr Faulkner's voice was quite hollow. 'Thank you, Mr Beech.'

'Speak *up*, madam, we cannot *hear* you. Ah! Thank you, Mrs Laurent,' and he leaned forward, 'do get her to speak up.'

'Yes, your worship,' and she turned to the woman in the dock. 'Speak up, dear,' and after the pause, 'and do answer the questions put to you.'

'What questions?'

Mr Beech thundered it out. 'Where is your son *now?* What is his full name? And do speak up, please.'

'Come closer, dear,' Mrs Laurent said, and linked arms. Mrs Kavanagh looked up. 'He's very good, your worship.'

'Yes, yes, yes, but do go on, madam.'

'Yes, sir.'

'Mrs Laurent!' She drew nearer to the bench.

'I think she should be taken out for a few minutes. She doesn't look very well to me. Anything new you can tell me about her?'

'Nothing. She's a nuisance to herself.'

'She's a nuisance to this court,' and he fixed his gaze on the woman in the dock. 'Why are you here again?'

'I was just asking some people how they were, sir, and the constable arrested me.'

'You do this kind of thing quite often?'

'Yes, sir. They looked nice people. I like nice people.'

'Yes, yes, yes. *Mrs* Laurent!' Mrs Laurent moved, Mrs Laurent paused.

'You don't appear to set any limits, madam,' Mr Faulkner said, and he seemed so close to Mrs Kavanagh that she closed eyes again.

'Why didn't you go home?'

'I had to think about it, sir.'

'They did their best,' whispered Mrs Laurent. 'Originally shared a small terraced house, since demolished.'

'Understood. I've nothing but admiration for your patience. She's no longer young. My clerk tells me there is no ship, and there is no son. The whole thing seems a delusion, Mrs Laurent.'

'Yes, your worship. It's a dream, really, but it helps.' Mr Faulkner wanted to explode, but refrained.

'She's in and out as regular as the clock. Is there nothing at all that can be done?'

'We've all tried,' Mrs Laurent replied.

'That might well be the trouble,' he said, and turned to Mrs Kavanagh. 'Mrs Kavanagh. I want you to tell us more about yourself. We want to help you. Your face is becoming too familiar here. Have you no friends?'

'Mrs Biddulph.'

'Is *that* all?'

'I've my son, sir, and sometimes I write to him. Things will be different when he comes home.'

'I hope so.'

And the clerk said, 'Six appearances in as many months. She's a problem.'

'You're a *problem*, madam,' cried Mr Faulkner.

'Yes, sir.' Mr Beech's thin lips parted, as if to smile, but Mr Faulkner waited only for the words.

'Regular visitor here, even in Mr Benson's time. He used to refer to her as his aunt,' and the smile followed. Unsmiling, and icily, Mr Faulkner exclaimed, 'Indeed!'

'Always says her son will pay the fine,' Mr Beech said.

'Taxes my patience.'

'She can be very trying.' Mr Faulkner wasn't listening, and he called again. 'Mrs Laurent.'

'She lived alone for years, and nobody knows anything about her . . .'

'Mrs Biddulph?'

'Two of a kind, your worship.'

'Was she really drunk on this occasion?'

'Not really, though I thought it unusual.'

'How so?'

'She's so often drunk.'

'A passion for it.'

'Yes, your worship.'

'Very difficult.'

'She was in a home on two occasions. Then finally the council found her this flat after they demolished her home.'

'I *see*. Can *nothing* be done?' Mrs Laurent sighed, and he heard it distinctly. 'We *try*,' she said.

'Of course, of course, Mrs Laurent. I'll adjourn for an hour. Please take her out.'

'Yes, your worship.'

'Extraordinary,' thought Mr Faulkner. 'Poor creature.' A door opened, and a door banged.

'Call the next case.'

'CALL THE NEXT CASE.'

*

Beyond the door, where the echoes lived, Mrs Laurent took the woman's arm, and led her slowly away. 'Come along,' she said.

'I'm coming.' Once she stopped dead, to look back, then half turned, to listen.

'Come *along*.'

'Where are you taking me?'

'In here,' Mrs Laurent said, opened a door, and gently pushed the woman into the room. 'Sit down. Cup of tea in a minute.'

'Thank you.' She sat down beside her.

'We *are* trying to help you.'

'Thank you.'

'No need to go on thanking me,' and at that moment the tea came. 'Drink it slowly. There's no hurry. Nobody wants you, and nobody is waiting. Something will have to be done, dear.'

'Will it?'

'*Yes*.' And the shout surprised her. 'Oh dear! I'm sorry,' Mrs Kavanagh said.

'The gentlemen want to help you.'

'Do they?' When the abrupt question came, the woman dropped the cup.

'Oh God,' she said, and again, 'I'm sorry.'

'Where is your son's ship *now*?'

'In some Indian ocean,' they said.

Mrs Laurent felt a tug on her arm, bent low for the message. '*Yes*?'

'He lives in my head,' Mrs Kavanagh said.

'*I* see. *I* understand.' Mrs Laurent studied the woman at her side, then said casually, 'You could do with a new coat. Would you like one?'

'I don't know.'

'I'm sure you would.'

'I'm not sure.'

'What *are* you sure about then?'

'Why don't they leave me alone?' A sudden aggressiveness, not lost on Mrs Laurent.

'Who are *they*?' A momentary silence, and then, 'I'll manage,' Mrs Kavanagh said.

'Good.' The woman sipped slowly at her second cup of tea.

'Won't be long now.' Where did she come from? *Where*? When? How old *was* she? *Was* there a son? Where lay the root? And what lay behind the days before yesterday? Mrs Laurent wondered about it, and then Mrs Kavanagh exclaimed very abruptly, 'D'you know what?'

'What, dear?'

'They once gave my friend Mrs Biddulph, three months, just for telling the truth.'

'*Did* they indeed?'

'Yes. They *did*.' Mrs Laurent caught the sharp tone of the voicc, a woman waking up, alcrt on a thrcshold.

'How long have you been at Totall Point?'

'Long enough.' A smile, and then, 'How long is long enough?'

'In the sky you mean?'

'Yes.'

'Said it then. Long enough.'

'Tell me about yourself.'

'What?'

'*Any*thing.'

'Oh! I see,' Mrs Kavanagh replied, but the questions confused her.

'How old is your son? Is he short or tall, fair or dark, what does he look like?'

'Black hair, and he's *really* tall. He has a big lick of hair on his forehead that won't stay back, sort of lives there.'

'Just fancy that.'

'Yes.'

'Is it a good ship, Mrs Kavanagh?'

'A nice ship.'

'Good.'

'I write him once a week. My friend Mrs Biddulph always posts the letters. Funny address really. *M.V. Devonian*, c/o GPO London.'

' 'Tis odd.'

'Drink up your tea.'

'Thank you,' and the Laurent smile was renewed.

'Why did you leave Afton House, Mrs Kavanagh?'

'Not very nice there. There was a woman in the next bed to me and she was always laughing, never stopped, *always* at it, I didn't like that very much. Liked where I was last Christmas . . .'

'Yes, yes,' Mrs Laurent said, waiting, for the moment, the revealing words.

'Somebody knocking,' Mrs Kavanagh said, and Mrs Laurent went to the door.

'Yes?'

'Mrs Laurent?'

'What is it,' following which Mrs Kavanagh became somewhat intrigued at a whispered conference just inside the door.

'Right,' the visitor said, and closed the door after him. Mrs Laurent sat down beside her charge. 'We're going home,' she said.

'Don't they want me then?'

'No. In the morning. Come along now,' and she assisted Mrs Kavanagh to her feet. 'Let's go,' and she led her out once more into the long, draughty corridor.

'You needn't take me home,' Mrs Kavanagh said. 'I know the way, thank you,' and pulled clear of her companion.

'I'll see you to the bus,' Mrs Laurent said.

'I know the way, thank you.' She led the woman across the road.

'I'll come for you tomorrow.'

'Will you?'

And then the bus pulled up, and Mrs Kavanagh got on, waved a hand, did not return the smile, and sat down in the corner. The bus dropped her off at Totall Point, and she stood at the kerb's edge, waiting, watching, and the traffic that never seemed to pause for a moment, whirled by. She had always dreaded the traffic lights. Others joined her, waiting. The lights flashed, and suddenly she moved.

'Wait,' and the voice behind her made her jump, as she lunged into the road, staggered.

'Don't want to be *killed*, do you?'

And softly over her shoulder, she replied, 'No, sir.'

'Well go on, woman, go *on*.'

'Yes, sir,' she said, and went on, confused and frightened, and when she reached the other side she turned and looked at the man behind her, had a fugitive vision of tallness, long legs, a swinging umbrella and briefcase. Unknown to her the world was screaming at him to hurry up, since the world, sharp as blades, refused to wait. She looked up at him, then uttered her usual prayer of the day.

'Sorry sir, thank you,' but the man had flashed away to the distance. The hands were hidden in the pockets, and she carried no bag. And there towering above her, the concrete, home. 'Ah!' she said. 'Ah!' Mrs Laurent had taken the next bus, and now followed behind her as she entered the building.

'Wait, Mrs Kavanagh,' she cried, and the woman turned, was rock still in a moment.

'What's the matter?'

'Come along,' Mrs Laurent said, took her arm, walked her towards the lift. A red light glimmered over the door.

'Come now,' and she gently pushed the woman into the lift. It whirred them skywards.

'You are high,' she said.

'Yes.' The lift stopped, they got out, and Mrs Laurent was at once authoritative. 'Key, dear,' then impatiently added, 'the *key*.'

'That's right,' and she opened the door, and pushed Mrs Kavanagh in.

'There! Home!'

'Thank you.'

'You don't look well, dear.'

The reply was direct, stubborn. 'I'm all right. I can manage.'

'You can't manage,' Mrs Laurent replied, stared round the cold, empty room.

'I *always* managed.'

'Come.' They stood by the table. 'Sit down.'

'You fuss too much,' Mrs Kavanagh said.

'Tut! tut!' and Mrs Laurent rushed around, switched on the light, then the fire, called out, 'I'll make tea.' Mrs Kavanagh, crouched in the chair, said nothing. And she quietly watched the woman fuss around her.

'Come along now,' and she was on her feet again, being quickly led down the room to the bed. She removed Mrs Kavanagh's hat and coat.

'There! You must lie down, dear. You're not well,' and she settled the pillows and rushed off again to make the tea. At the cupboard she called out, 'have you anything in a bottle?'

'In the cupboard. Rum.'

'Good.' At which Mrs Kavanagh lay back, slowly closed her eyes.

'I *am* tired,' she said.

'Of course you are.' Mrs Laurent went to the window and looked out and then down. She turned quickly away and rushed off to make the tea. 'You all right?' And the woman in the bed called back, 'I can manage.' She sat up when Mrs Laurent arrived with the tray.

'That's right,' settling her, after which she sat by the bed, poured tea, added a tot from the flask. 'There!'

'Thank you.' Mrs Laurent sat quietly stirring her own. 'Feel better now?'

'Said I always managed,' Mrs Kavanagh replied, supped again.

'Nice,' she added.

'Mrs Kavanagh.'

'Yes?'

'Tell me something. Why do you always get drunk? Every pension day the same? The reply was prompt, wholly unexpected.

'Better than being sober,' Mrs Kavanagh said, even offered a smile. 'Know who you are when you're sober. Horrible sometimes.' And quite involuntarily, Mrs Laurent stuttered, 'How extraordinary.' She stared about the room, noting a general untidiness, remembered an entrance that was cold, the window, and looking down and down and down.

'More tea, Mrs Kavanagh?'

'No, thank you,' and she tendered her cup, then lay back again.

'That's right. You've had a trying day.' There was complete silence. 'Are you asleep, dear?' The woman was fully stretched on the bed, seemed scarcely breathing. Mrs Laurent drew the overcoat higher, bent over her, 'You *are* all right?'

'Told you. I manage. I always manage.' She watched her carrying the tray up the room, heard her washing up.

'I'll be going soon,' said Mrs Laurent. And still the silence. 'Poor thing,' she thought, suddenly realized she had fallen asleep. Perhaps she ought to go now, but didn't, returning to the bed, sitting down again, watching. Mrs Kavanagh stirred.

'You've had a nice little nap,' she said.

'Oh! Have I? Yes, of course. I did fall asleep.'

'Don't sit up.'

'No.'

'What time is your friend coming?'

'She won't be long.' Mrs Laurent got up, walked slowly down the room, went to the window again. The light was falling.

'I'll draw the curtains,' she said.

'*Leave* them.'

'Very well,' replied Mrs Laurent, still stood staring out, turned and came slowly down the room. Mrs Kavanagh watched, thought of somebody moving in and out of light and darkness.

'I'll be going shortly.'

'What for?'

'Will Mrs Biddulph be long?'

'Don't know, really, sometimes she just comes, sometimes she doesn't. Depends.'

'Depends on what, dear?'

'Mrs Biddulph never says.' Mrs Laurent glanced at her watch. 'I'll wait a little longer.'

'*Told* you I can manage, always managed.'

'What does your friend Mrs Biddulph do?'

'*Nothing*,' and nothing seemed more final.

'You *must* lie down,' Mrs Laurent said. 'That's better.' She glanced at her watch again, wondered when the woman would arrive and then she felt Mrs Kavanagh's hand in her own, a pressure there, the signal, 'don't go.'

'She's late.' Silence.

'Are you asleep?' Silence. Thread-like, faint, the words floated in the air, reached Mrs Laurent's ear.

'I hope that Mr Faulkner lets me stay.'

'Thought you were asleep.'

'Wasn't.'

'Thought you were. You were very quiet.'

'Sometimes I lie here, and I listen to it.'

'Listen to what, dear?'

'The silence,' the voice was suddenly stronger, the bed creaked.

'Wish your friend would hurry up.'

'She'll come. Always comes. She's my friend.'

'All right,' Mrs Laurent said, sighed a little, checked the watch. 'I'm glad you have such a good friend.'

'Nice to have a friend,' Mrs Kavanagh said, hugging the word. 'Always comes on this evening, writes the letter for me. Sometimes I just want to write the letter myself, and then somehow I can't be bothered, worries me that, I mean not wanting to when I *should*. And Mrs Laurent said nothing, and heard nothing save the words of a man in a distant place.

'There is no ship. There is no son.'

'Feed the dream,' she thought, 'there's nothing else,' remembering the one single occasion when she had written the imaginary letter for Mrs Kavanagh, sealing and stamping it, and then, leaving her, stood at balcony's edge and shredded it and let it float into the void where all delusionary letters are finally posted. And sat there, hands folded, staring at this woman, and the silence around them, and the light continuing to fall. Mrs Kavanagh stared back, and waited, wondered.

'Yes,' Mrs Laurent thought, 'the son is made of paper, and the words wind round and about an old woman's brain.'

Then most abruptly, and again she was low over the woman in the bed: 'It might be best if your friend didn't come, Mrs Kavanagh. You need sleep, you are tired, and you're not well.' Mrs Kavanagh sat up at once, pointed an accusing finger, and asked, 'Why are you looking at me like that?'

'Not looking at you, dear, just thinking.'

'Oh!'

'She's late.'

'She won't be long now, I'm sure. Can go if you want. I'll manage.'

'Who lives next door?'

'Wintens.'

'Tell me about them.'

'He's market, and she's office cleaning.'

'Are they nice neighbours?'

'They're all right, I suppose,' and Mrs Kavanagh shrugged them off. Mrs Laurent rose.

'You *are* going then?' Mrs Laurent picked up her raincoat, bag, and briefcase. '*Must*.' Mrs Kavanagh said, 'I see,' paused, and then in a loud voice, 'If that Mr Faulkner had given me a month for shaking hands with that man at the bus stop, I'd've been glad.'

'I can't answer that, and I don't understand you,' Mrs Laurent said. The woman gave a curious little laugh, saying, 'I cross my fingers every time.'

And the balm followed, 'Of course you do.'

'You still there?'

'I'm here,' and again hand touched hand.

'I think you've had another cat nap,' Mrs Laurent said.

'I was having a dream, I think. I like dreaming sometimes.'

'D'you have many visitors?'

'Sometimes, if I'm here.'

'It is your home.'

'*Is* it?'

'Mrs Biddulph isn't *coming*,' Mrs Laurent said.

'Funny then. Always does if she says she is.'

'Why don't you lie down and rest.'

'Don't go . . . yet.'

'Do lie *down*.'

'You're angry.'

'I'm not,' replied Mrs Laurent. 'And tomorrow will be a very long day indeed unless you get a good night's sleep.'

'Don't tell me about it, don't tell me anything. Just leave me alone. Sometimes I'm glad, and sometimes I'm not.'

'What about, dear?'

'Everything.'

'It's all right. I'm still here.'

'Thank you.'

'Don't like leaving you like this, Mrs Kavanagh. Tell me, did you have breakfast this morning?'

'I managed.'

'Now I *must* go. I'll drop in on the Wintens on my way out, dear.'

Mrs Kavanagh had turned her face to the wall. There was no reply. There was nothing that could come. Mrs Laurent bent over her again. Was she asleep? Wasn't she? And then she was more fully aware of the silence, the loneliness of this room. 'Poor creature.'

'Mrs Kavanagh!' So she bent lower over the bed, listened again. 'Good,' she thought, and drew away, once more surveyed the room. And looking at her watch she told herself that Mrs Biddulph would not come. She switched off the fire, went to the window, drew the curtains. She put a finger to the light switch, and then withdrew it, tiptoed to the door and went out, closed it quietly behind her, listened for the click. She stood outside the door for a moment or two.

'I'll ask next door to keep an eye on her,' and rang the bell.

Eddy opened up. 'Yes?'

'Mr Winten?'

'Right.'

'I've just brought Mrs Kavanagh home,' she began, but Eddy knew.

'Understood,' he said.

'You'll keep an eye on her then?'

'Yes.'

'Good of you. Here's her key.'

'Thank you.'

'Good night,' Eddy said, and stood there watching her walk away into the semi-darkness of the corridor.

*

It was at this moment that the lights went out, and the world, inside as well as out, was plunged into darkness. The woman in the bed stirred slightly, woke, half opened her eyes and closed them again, stiffened, clutched the bedsheet, listened. The silence was total.

'Oh God!' she exclaimed. 'Where am I? What time is it? Must've been dreaming, sat up, lay down again. What time is it?' There was no answer. 'Anybody *there*?' And then the dropped voice, the whisper. 'Don't panic, Brigid, don't panic.' Wanting to get up, to move, and afraid to, wanting to call out and dreading the answer. And the light. What on earth had happened to the light? And again she pressed hands to her eyes.

'The bloody *dark*.' The voice broke. 'Did it happen? When? How long have I been here? Was I dreaming?' And shouted into the empty room, 'It's like being lost.'

Slowly, carefully, she got off the bed, came erect, clasped hands, and listened again. The same silence. 'I must *do* something, I must,' and didn't, instead knelt, stiff and still, one hand gripping the bedclothes. She put a finger to her lips, felt the tremble of them, and then exclaimed, loud into the darkness, 'She never came. Lena never came.' She flung out her arms, groped the air about. 'I must get up, I must go and see, check the light, I must find the door, the *door*.' She moved, first one foot and then the other, toppled, and lay on the floor, her hands half smothering the word that came free.

'*Why*? Had she come? Hadn't she?' And all this darkness and silence, so sudden, what did it mean, as she half rose and fell again, and began to crawl away from the bed. 'Oh God! I'm lost.' The silence frightened, the darkness seemed endless. She knelt, clasped hands again, and waited, and listened, and wondered. And then she knew that she was totally alone.

'I wasn't dreaming, it's *real*.' She must get to the light switch, she must get to the fire, and began to move again, always listening, and groping, and waiting for the knock that might come. Kneeling, she felt the hardness of wood beneath her.

'What was that?' And listened and waited and wondered. 'I'm afraid. I am. I am.' In a moment it was there, under the door, the first sound.

'Not again, oh Christ, not *again*.'

After the wind came, after the fang in it began scratching under the door. She lay flat on the floor, covered her head with her hands, pressed hard. It wasn't the silence, nor the darkness, nor the knock that had refused to come. It was the sound under the door. It was the first message, and she knew what to do. She came slowly to her feet, moving again, slowly, carefully, towards what she thought must be the window, bumped into a chair, cried out, 'the chair', then suddenly realized she was standing at the table in the centre of the room, and clung to it, listening again, waiting. She groped on, her hands stretched out before her, to feel, to find, and found it, the window, suddenly felt the warmth of curtains in her hands.

'Thank God for that,' and was still again, rooted. Yes, the window was there, and it kept outside the solid bank of darkness that lay beyond it. And she knew now that she was a prisoner of the darkness, inside and out. 'The clock! The clock!' she cried, wondering where it was, if only she could hear the tick. Had she remembered to wind it? If she could just *hear* it ticking, the sound would be very reassuring. But the darkness held her fast, and again she was thinking of the door. Perhaps it would be almost a voyage to reach it, and moved again, this time backwards, and hit the chair, and collapsed into it, saying 'Ah!' as she heavily sat, which was all of the relief she felt at that moment, finding it again, and without too much doddering. She sat, crouched, hugged the warmth into herself. She knew the cold was there, in the stillness, the sound of her own breathing the only anchor in the darkness. She was still in the room, alone, and the silence wrapped about her. Again she closed her eyes and listened. The cold of the room was seeking her bone, and she knew it. Was that the clock? Ticking. And where had she left it, and *had* she wound it? The ticks now would sound like the footsteps of approaching friends. She shivered, was conscious of it, and cried loud into the room, 'The door! The door!' *Had* she closed it? Groping again. Where on earth had it got to? The chair was there, and she was in it. At first the darkness had merely been confusing, indifferent, obliterating. The silence. That was it, the silence. Should she get up, go and see, *feel*, for the knob, the bolt, the door? Or should she just sit quietly, with closed eyes, sit still as still and wait. Placing her hands flat upon her knees she began fiercely to rub them, her ear ever alert for the tick of the lost clock. And then she heard the first sound, and realized what it really was, accepted it, and bent even lower in the chair.

'Where am I?' she cried.

But the room refused to answer. There was no message, and there was no meaning, and she moved again. The room was dark, the world was dark, and nothing to think about save the door, nothing to listen for save the tick of the clock, which at that moment, died. It was some time before she realized this, and there was the single moment of terror when she did, for now it refused to tell her where it was, and it had always told her. Often she had listened to it talking to her, telling her where it was, there when she went out, and there when she returned. It told her that the room was total, and that she was in it. But now it could not say whether a door was opened or closed, whether the light, too, had drowned. The very breath of panic was with her. 'Oh God!' And the hurricane of words in her ears.

'Where am I? What *is* the time? How long has it been dark? How soon will it be light? And where is the *door*?' and followed this with a low scream, 'The door, the door,' paused a moment, and then the words of stone, 'I mustn't panic, mustn't.'

The cold was silent as it crept, sought, clawed. Suddenly she realized that she could no longer move, that she had ceased to wonder, was hidden, lost. When the sound returned, she strained to listen, listened. At first it seemed like the lightest rustling of papers, and then like the sudden swish of a skirt, and later still, it felt like a foot's fall. The sound broke a stillness in her, and in a moment she had forgotten the cold. Gripping her knees, she rocked gently to and fro in the chair, and fell again, her face to the floor, and the sound of her own breathing was like a wave of the sea.

'What shall I *do*?'

'Feel me,' said the cold.

'Find me,' said the door.

'Remember me,' said the darkness, as she moved, as she half rose, knelt, crawled again.

She felt herself moving forward, and something appeared to lightly brush her face, and it wasn't the cold, nor blackness of room. Into her cupped hands she whispered, 'It's the door, of course, the door.' And again the sound. 'It's coming through, it's coming *in*, it is, it is,' and then was conscious of the draught at her feet.

Always she had closed her door, locked it, and never forgot. *Was* it open? Had Mrs Laurent forgotten to close it, properly, tightly, securely? And where *was* it? Yes. 'That's it, of course, it's *me*. I didn't quite close it, I didn't,' and then it leapt out. 'Listen!' she cried, and listened. When she heard it she thought that something was coming to an end, and once more was stiff and rooted where she stood. It had come, and it had been coming all along, had found its way out of the world that was dark, and could have no meaning until it had died by light. It had sighed, and whispered, and whimpered, had sucked its way in, was *there*. It had danced in the corridors. Up and down, and round and about, restless, tireless, and it could not get in. The doors were closed against it. It leapt forward, receded, returned again, and on its wings the cold that now frightened the woman in the chair. She had not moved, dared not.

'I must. I must close it.' Her best friend had always been the light. 'I must *move*,' and could not.

'Don't,' said the cold.

'Wait,' said the darkness. And the room cried into her ear, 'This is where you are, and you are in it, your home,' and it was lone, and it was final.

It was all right before, everything was, moments ago,

minutes ago. Perhaps it was hours. She did not know. The darkness never gave up, never ceased to press, and she thought of the light, and prayed for it. The room buried and terrified, and she shouted wildly, 'The door!'

The words leapt into the silence, save for the wind that still whistled, and found, and stayed. She longed for a single finger in the darkness, the clock, and the tick of it. Always when she heard it she knew where she was. Knew it now as she felt the draught at her back, and moved again, blindly, hands pawing air, and at last found it. Not shut, but a fraction open.

'She never *closed* it properly,' angry, furious, and always frightened. When she pressed her back against it, it did not at first move, and she pressed again, and finally heard the click. She fell again, lay there. 'At last! God! If only the light would come, if only the wind would die down,' and was on her knees again, almost without realizing it. And finally stuttered out, 'I don't understand.' She thought of yesterday, but tomorrow seemed whole deserts away. Between the twin pressures of loneliness and aberration, the calm moment came, and she thought of her friend, wondered why she had not come, the one that counted in a whole pyramid of lives that crowded about her days.

'I must get up.'

If only she could get back to the bed, find it, clutch it, reach up, lie on it, quiet and safe. Yes, she would lie quietly there and wait. There seemed nothing else to do.

'I'll call, I must shout,' and the panic returning, back, right back, smothering, confounding. 'I will.' And then she was crying softly to herself, and felt a strange relief from this, yet wondered why she had, she who so rarely cried. The masthead in her wavered, the ship tossed. 'Oh no! Not now, not now,' and blubbered into cupped hands, and started to go forward again, to where the bed was, might be, had always been. If she heard someone, if she heard something, *anything*, but there remained only the single sound, and the cold that was in it. Try being calm, and stop wondering, wondering. The bed. She must find the bed. She ached for the feel of it, the safety there.

'What was *that*?' She pressed the flat of her hands to her ears, was afraid again. The whispers dragged from the tongue.

'What is it? Who's there?' she asked, but only heard the heart's thuds. 'Oh God, of course, I never thought of that. Perhaps somebody had come in, soundlessly, through the door that for some reason or other had refused to close. Perhaps someone is standing in the darkness at this very moment, listening, watching.' And cried in her mind, 'Don't panic.' Who? When? Where? Why? And shouted again, 'Who's there?' Her ears seemed only filled by the marauding sounds of the world. It was like that these days, it was the way it went.

'Anybody there?' And waited again, the words tossed into the blackness. She was conscious of her own sudden rage, the violent leap of it.

'Help me!' Doubt struck again, the hands flailed the air, and words on the tongue that now refused to come out.

If she could hear one single voice, one single footstep that would tell her where she was. The words hammered again.

'There's nobody here, I'm imagining it all, of course you closed the door, and the light will come on again. It must. It's just the surprise, the silence, and this waiting. *Why* didn't I keep the blanket in my hand, my coat, I'm sure there were matches in the pocket, I . . . but did I? How long am I kneeling here?'

'I'll shout again,' and didn't.

'The cold. I never noticed that, never.' So confusing, so

frustrating, and where on earth was her friend, now? What *had . . . hap*pened? Said she'd come, always comes, Lena never forgot.

'Poor Lena.'

She was crawling again, almost without realizing it. And as she crawled she thought of the world, her days. And of yesterday, and what was in it, and what had fallen out of it. That long walk back from a known place. Plodding, and dodging the feet, the mad flying feet of people that never once looked back. There seemed no hurry here, in the darkness that stretched further and further. She remembered the great confusions of travel, from one road and street to another, the shouts in her ears that were automatic in the round of her days. And walking again, and resolute, and knowing where to go, what to do, remembering the lights, and the station, and the big welcoming face of the clock.

'She'll come, I'm sure Lena will come.' And then she found, and cried out, 'I've found it, thank God, I've found it,' and fell heavily against her bed, and lay there. At last.

And clinging to it, and climbing slowly into it, a collapse and a sigh, feeling the wood and the blanket and the pillow, the touch of friends.

'I'm glad! I'm glad.' She covered her head with the blanket. 'I wish . . . I wish.' Again the wind, and the voice in it, 'Listen,' and she could not shut it out.

'Wait,' the darkness said, 'just wait.' She sank deeper into the bed. She thought she would open her eyes, under the blanket, in the warmth there, and did not.

'The lights can't be gone forever. They'll come back soon.' Waiting and waiting. 'Lena,' she thought, 'Lena,' she said.

Lena loomed, was large, close in a moment. Once, they had been very close, perhaps forever, until someone they had neither seen nor heard had said 'No!' ever since which the world was different. And out of the darkness rose a wall that was familiar, a gate, and a door. 'A pity, a great pity. We were happy then.'

Slowly her head came clear of the blanket, and in a flash she had forgotten Lena, was back, where the silence was, the cold, and the darkness that would not lift.

'Who's *there*?' a demented moment.

And the ache that she had not noticed was suddenly there, and she thought, 'The light's gone, it'll never come back, never.' On hands and knees she dragged herself away from the bed, and the cold followed after.

'If I could find my *coat*. The matches . . .' The moment she bumped into the obstruction, she had the answer.

'The chair, I've found the chair,' and cried with the relief of it. She sat, tentatively at first, clung, and finally sank into it.

'I'll just sit here, and wait,' and huddled there, gripping the arms of the chair tightly, and then once again became aware of the sound under the door.

'Wait,' said the darkness.

'Listen,' the wind said. But she did not wait, and she did not listen. She thought she would open her eyes, and did not, and when the light came she did not see it, nor the closed door of a room that now appeared to have neither beginning nor end. When the building moved she screamed inside herself, high in the sky.

'Lena!'

And thought of Lena, and now knew that she would not come. When the door rattled she flung herself to the floor, a duty to do, a duty to be remembered. The eyes tightly closed, the finger tips pressed fiercely into the ears. In the absence of anything else she talked to herself.

'Where *is* Lena? Now?' Heard the Laurent words. 'See you tomorrow. Get a good night's sleep. You look tired.'

'Mrs Laurent's gone,' she said, and heard the word 'gone' echo in her ear.

'Was that a knock? No,' and stiffened where she lay. 'I wish . . .' And cried aloud, 'Who's that?' Listened again, and there was nothing.

'I'm imagining things. Oh God! I wish I knew what time it is.' Lena was back, was there, she saw her loom, and the words were there, yet refused to come.

'I wish I knew, I wish . . .'

The sudden tapping on the door was too much, and she cried out, 'Leave me alone.' She turned over on her back, threw wide her arms, stared skywards.

'The light! The light!'

'You all right, dear?' Lil said, softly, behind the door.

'Who is it?'

'Me?' An age passed, and then she heard it, a key in the lock.

'Mrs Kavanagh,' Lil said, 'Are you . . . ?' knelt where she lay.

'Where am I?' The arms about her, and a known voice.

'It's all *right*, dear.' Lil put an arm more tightly round her, raised her up. The eyes so tightly closed slowly opened, and she saw fear and distrust.

'There! There! It's all *right*,' Lil said.

The leaden words hit the room. 'Is it?'

'It's always like this when the wind comes,' Lil said.

'Is it?' And bewilderment was fully home.

'We were worried about you, dear. Mrs Laurent left us the key, just in case. Eddy was worried too.'

'Was he? She didn't come, and she said she would,' Mrs Kavanagh said, her tone of voice accusing, aggressive.

'Come along,' Lil said, 'you can't stay here like this,' and got her to her feet, as she listened to the wind again, as she was happy about the returning light.

'Thank you.'

'Forget it.'

'You *are* a good friend,' Mrs Kavanagh said, tried to smile, smiled.

'I was all right till the lights went out.'

'Yes, yes . . . come along, dear,' and Lil led her slowly down the room.

'Every time the wind comes I cross my fingers.'

'Don't we all?'

'I *was* frightened,' Mrs Kavanagh said. And the balm followed. 'Of course you were. There now,' and she heard the door click behind her, and there at the door was Eddy, waiting.

'She all right, Lil?'

'Scared stiff.'

'Poor old . . .'

'That's right,' Lil said, and ushered the woman into the room. 'Come and sit down,' then turned to Eddy, 'Eddy!' and Eddy knew what that meant, and disappeared into the kitchen.

'I was all right till then,' Mrs Kavanagh said, looked shyly at the girl next door. 'I was, *really*.'

Eddy returned, knelt, said quietly, 'Here you are, dear. Drink it,' and held the cup to her lips. After which she lay back in the chair. When she closed her eyes Eddy said, 'That's it,' and got up, took Lil's arm, went into the bedroom. They both sat, and conspiratorial whispers followed.

'She's not herself at all,' Eddy said.

'I know. And she has to go to that court again.'

'*Again?*'

'Yes. Adjourned till tomorrow,' Lil said.

'How stupid can you get? She ought to be in bed, who's her doctor?' Lil didn't know, nobody knew.

'Her friend never turned up.'

'Better have the spare room.'

'I'll see to it in a minute,' Lil said, on which Eddy left the room, returned a few minutes later with tea, a bottle, two glasses.

'Scared me *stiff*,' Eddy said, and so abruptly that it parted Lil's lips, but nothing came out, and Eddy sealed it up with 'the bloody wind.'

'Ought never to be up this high, Lil.'

'They said she had to, and that's it, well isn't it?'

'Them again,' growled Eddy. 'Go and see how she is.' Eddy cursed 'them', and Lil went out. Lil sat close to the woman, Lil talked. She watched the eyes open.

'All right now?'

'I'll manage,' Mrs Kavanagh said, the old words again. 'Thank you.'

'Eddy's fixed the spare room, dear. You can sleep there till the morning.'

'Thank you.'

'I can't understand Mrs Biddulph,' Lil said, 'she nearly always comes.'

'I *know*,' and the words hollow.

'I never heard you come back,' Lil said.

'Never heard myself come back when it started. Really knocked me.'

'You'll be yourself again after a good night's sleep,' Lil said.

'Thank you.' A quiet smile from Lil, and a quick 'tut! tut!'

'Ready?' she asked.

'I'm all right now,' Mrs Kavanagh said, tried to rise, rose, and Lil led her away to the spare room. 'Come along now, dear,' and she removed the woman's big coat, slowly undressed her, put her to bed. 'There!'

'Ah!' Mrs Kavanagh said, 'Oh! . . .,' and the slightest smile between the words. And slowly, and dragged, as she clutched the hand held out to her, '*Such* a mercy that the lights came on again.'

Bent over the bed, Lil said, 'And now they're going off again. Sleep tight,' and she switched out the light. She walked slowly to the door, turned, and stood there, listening. 'Good night!'

'Good . . .'

She closed the door quietly. Eddy rose the moment she walked in.

'Late,' he said, and switched off the television set.

'Eddy?'

'What?'

'I never knew Mrs Kavanagh's been in and out of prison for years.'

'The world knows,' replied Eddy.

'Awful,' she said. 'Some things are. Should never have sent her to a place like this.'

'Mad,' Eddy said, 'quite mad. Her old place is still standing up after three years, she was all right there.'

'They both were.'

'Of course,' blurted Eddy. 'I forgot. They were both there.' He strained for Lil's words.

'That's right,' she said, very casually.

'What'll they do with her, d'you think, Lil?'

'God knows.'

'What about her people?' he asked.

'Hasn't any.'

'Oh! I see.'

'She's not London.'

'*Isn't* she?'

'Irish as shamrock,' Lil said.

'Poor woman.'

'Her flat's a mess,' Lil said.

'Give it a bit of a tidy up before she goes back in the morning, yes?'

'Yes. I'll do that.'

'Good,' he said, 'come on then,' and pulled her to her feet, and they left the room. Eddy looked carefully round, then switched off the light. He stood a moment at the door of the spare room, listened.

'Well away,' he said, 'poor old thing.' They undressed, they lay, they did not switch off the light.

'Lil?' and she turned to him.

'How about a weekend with Betty. Be a bit of a change.'

'I'll think about it, dear.'

'Good. Good.'

'Eddy?' and they were closer then.

'What?'

'Know what she told me?'

'What?'

'She wants to go back in.'

'In where?'

'Prison.'

'Good God! Must be cracked, Lil.'

'Meant it.'

'Then she *is* cracked.'

'Sad.'

'About Betty?' he said.

'I *said* I'd think about it, *didn't* I?'

Eddy stretched in the bed, closed his eyes. He hadn't an answer. 'Nervy,' he thought, and more fiercely, 'We're all nervy when this bloody building starts shaking.' He held her hand, he kissed her.

'All right, old girl, it's all right. Understood,' and Lil said nothing. 'Upsets everybody,' he said, and she said nothing, and he understood that, too. She was like that sometimes, lying so still and quiet in the bed, staring up at the ceiling, her hands behind her head, and her mouth tightly closed against the words that might come, explode, rock Eddy. He felt his hand squeezed, he turned to her again, and she put a finger across his lips and said quietly, 'Ssh!' And Eddy shushed.

'The light,' she said. He jerked violently beside her. 'OK Lil,' and they were in darkness. They seemed closer then, and they listened to that which would not stop, was *there*, so they were mindful of it, and the clock's tick, and the silence from the next room. They wondered when it would cease.

'Lil.'

'What?'

'Oh! . . . nothing,' Eddy said, 'nothing at all, really.'

'Go asleep,' she said.

'Nighty night.' And again Lil said nothing.

'There! It's stopped now, Lil,' Eddy said. And Lil said nothing.

*

This building has six corridors leading down to the world. And four hundred front doors that are closed, and eight hundred and sixty windows, and three hundred and seventy-five faces behind them, and the roof nudges the clouds.

III

'Come along,' Mrs Laurent said, and she came along.

'Brigid Kavanagh.'

She linked arms with Mrs Laurent, they went on down, past the odd smile, the stares, picking up the words that were worn.

'One of your old customers.'

'Regular as clockwork.'

'Clings like ivy.' The door opened, and the door closed.

'Good luck,' Mrs Laurent said, but Mrs Kavanagh made no reply. And Mr Faulkner was waiting.

'Bring the defendant a little nearer,' he said, 'she's rather deaf.'

'Forward.' And she went forward.

'You are Mrs Kavanagh?'

'Yes, sir.'

'You are charged with being drunk and disorderly, and making a nuisance. Have you anything to say?'

'Nothing.'

'Have you anything to *say*?'

Mrs Laurent looked up. 'She says no, your worship.'

Adjusting his spectacles, Mr Faulkner said, 'You are an old customer.' Titters.

'*Silence!*'

'You came out a month ago?'

'Yes, sir.'

'What *is* your age, madam?'

'Sixty.'

'Have you a *family*?'

'One son.'

'And where is he, madam?'

'I *told* you. On a ship, sir.'

'Is he at present afloat?'

'Yes, sir.'

Near sing-song, Mr Faulkner said, '*I* . . . see,' and the voice was tired.

'About bail, your worship?' whispered the clerk.

'*None*.'

'*Mrs* Kavanagh?'

'Yes, sir.'

'I want you to pay attention to what I have to say.' He paused a moment. 'You do fully understand me?'

'Yes, sir.'

'Speak up, please.'

'I said "yes" to your worship.'

'Your record of petty offences is a long one. I have been studying the records. I was trying to discover if there was any point at which I could help you.' Silence.

'Can you *hear* me?'

'Yes, sir.'

'You have been in and out of prison for forty years, madam. Time and again you have made promises that you have never kept. For some reason, unknown to me, you find yourself quite unable to keep them.' There was a long pause. The court waited.

'You are no sooner out of prison than you are in the public house. You have a home, and Mrs Laurent has seen it. On more occasions than I care to mention you have been helped. And you have also been warned of the consequences . . .'

'Why don't you forgive her, and be *done* with it.'

'Remove that woman from the court.'

'Remove that . . .' and gibberish in tow.

'This court has always been ready to help you. I understand you have no relatives, beyond this son at present at sea. Have you no friends?'

'Mrs Biddulph,' woodenly.

'Where is she now?'

'I don't know, sir.'

'Why don't you *do* something . . . ?'

'*Out*side,' the usher said, towering, pushing towards the exit. Mr Faulkner leaned close to Mr Beech. 'I shall not commit her.'

'Yes, your worship.'

'*Ill.*'

'Still manages to get drunk.'

'Yes, your worship.'

'Her fame spreads. Distressing to see her returning here time and time again. I realize the son is a complete delusion.'

'She's a history to this court, your worship, a map with almost everything on it,' and Mr Beech smiled, and Mr Faulkner did not.

'Bring the defendant closer.'

'Forward.'

'Go along, dear,' Mrs Laurent said, gently pushed.

'All right where she was, your worship.'

'What councils do is hardly the business of this court, Mrs Laurent.'

'She lives alone.'

'We *know* she lives alone. Thank you, Mrs Laurent. *Mrs* Kavanagh!'

'Yes, sir.'

'Don't you *care*?'

'Care, sir?'

And Mr Beech shouted, '*Care*, madam!'

'For what?'

'Yourself,' Mr Faulkner said.

'Oh! Yes, sir, I do. I was quite happy till they took me. I always am, and then they take me. Even take my friend sometimes.'

'Imagined,' Mr Faulkner thought, 'like son and ship.' He subjected the woman to a long hard stare, and then said, very quietly, 'You are discharged,' after which he sat back, and closed his eyes.

'You're free, dear,' Mrs Laurent said.

'Can't hear.'

'You're *free*.'

She saw the woman wilt, took both her hands. 'Everything's all right, Mrs Kavanagh. Come along now.' But Mrs Kavanagh tore free of Mrs Laurent, covered her face, and quietly, began to cry. An arm about her, a soothing voice, 'Come along. You are *free*, dear.' The woman remained rooted where she stood, her face completely hidden behind her hands.

'Take her away,' Mr Beech said. The court was suddenly silent, the world waiting, and then the world heard it.

'I don't want to, I want to go *in*,' muffled through spread fingers.

'Please take her out,' Mr Faulkner said, and bit his lips, stared.

'Awful,' Mr Beech said, and Mr Faulkner said nothing. Mrs Laurent felt the tenseness, the hands pressed tight, took her arm.

'This way,' she said, final, authoritative. The hands fell, she looked, the court looked. 'I want to go in.' Under the breath an usher said, 'Oh God!' quietly helped Mrs Laurent remove the familiar face from the sight of the assembly. The door opened, and the door closed.

Mrs Laurent was irritated, and she was stunned.

'I hate him,' Mrs Kavanagh said, halted, was pulled on,

and close together, and very slowly they went down the corridor, the heavy footsteps and the echoes following. 'Don't *worry*.' Which made Mrs Kavanagh halt again, and she half turned and looked back and saw the closed doors.

'Here,' Mrs Laurent said, pressed a handkerchief into her hand.

'Th . . . thank . . .' and she blew her nose.

'There now,' Mrs Laurent said. 'Keep it. Come along,' and she came. They stopped, and the door opened. 'In there, dear.' The room was empty, but the fire was cheerful. They sat beside it.

'Would you like me to take you home, Mrs Kavanagh?'

'No.'

'I'd like to.'

'No. I *wouldn't*.' They were both silent, motionless. The door burst open, a man put his head in, cried 'Sorry,' and went off, the door slammed.

'Mrs Kavanagh!' Neither word nor movement, Mrs Kavanagh being closely locked up in Kavanagh world.

'You can't stay here, dear.' The woman did not answer, and they sat on, listened to the tick of a clock . . . 'Poor creature,' Mrs Laurent thought. 'I suppose there is such a thing as an end, rose to her feet, bent over the huddled, silent woman.

'Listen,' she said, 'listen.' Mrs Kavanagh looked up at her. Her mouth remained tightly shut, the eyes accusing.

'Wasn't much to ask for,' she said.

A steadiness had come back to the voice, as though the hour with the ice in it had vanished. Mrs Laurent was suddenly all authority, firm, yet gentle.

'I'll see you home. Come now.' She took the woman's arm, they left the room, bumped into a salutation or two in the corridor.

'Almost lives here,' a passing man said, and a fugitive grin

'Almost,' Mrs Laurent replied. They drew nearer to the light, and the world that was waiting for them.

'I know him,' Mrs Kavanagh said.

'He knows you, dear.' They paused at the entrance.

'I've a car.'

'I said no,' Mrs Kavanagh said, and Mrs Laurent gave a brisk nod of the head, thinking, 'What does one do in an extreme case?' searched for an answer.

'Sure?' she asked. Mrs Kavanagh gave her a withering glance. 'Said no, didn't I?'

'Of course you did, dear.'

'They could have let me in if they'd wanted to.'

There was no reply, and Mrs Laurent slowly descended the steps, her arm still linked in that of the woman. 'Wait!' and a hand in the air. The traffic tore by. She thought of Totall Point, the hidden world.

'Did your friend come last night?'

'No.'

'I'm sorry. I expect you'll see her this morning.'

'If she didn't come last night, she's bound to come in the morning. She's like that, Mrs Biddulph.'

'I'm glad.' And they crossed the road, stood waiting at the bus stop.

'Only take a few minutes to run you back, dear,' Mrs Laurent said, her eye fixed on the parked car. Mrs Kavanagh looked up, stared, and said nothing.

'Lonely, terribly lonely,' and Mrs Laurent knew that it wasn't the answer.

'I'll see you on the bus, dear.'

'You'll see me nowhere.'

'There's nothing more I can do then?'

'No.' The bus came, the bus went by, and the two women were still standing at the kerb's edge.

'Goodbye,' Mrs Laurent said, offered a quick smile, and added, 'I'll look you up shortly.'

'If you'd said one single word to Mr Faulkner he would have let me go back in.'

'Good*bye*, Mrs Kavanagh.'

There was no reply. Mrs Kavanagh turned her back on her companion, and started off down the long road. Mrs Laurent waved, Mrs Laurent called 'Good luck,' but the woman went stolidly on. Mrs Laurent still stood, watched the figure in the big coat become smaller and smaller until finally the distance swallowed her up. She quickly crossed the road, got into her car, drove away. Mrs Kavanagh's pace had slackened, and once or twice she veered towards a shop window, then violently outwards towards the kerb.

'Steady,' the man said, a hand gripping her arm. 'You all right?'

'I'm all right,' woodenly, not looking at the man. Mrs Kavanagh talked to Mrs Kavanagh. Her head was bent a little forward, she looked neither right nor left, and her hands remained buried deep in the big pockets of her coat. A Mrs Laurent appeared to block her path, but only for an instant.

'I suppose she's good, in *her* way.' The open door of The Marquis suddenly yawned at her. She went in. The place was empty, save for a barman busy behind the counter. He turned suddenly.

'Morning.'

'Morning.'

'Nice day.'

'Can I sit down?' Mrs Kavanagh said.

'If you want to,' casually.

'Thank you.'

He leaned across the counter, offered a smile. 'Get you anything?'

'Nothing,' and after a long pause, 'No thank you.' He whistled a tune, and the glasses tinkled. He had forgotten her. She rested her arms on the table, stared out into the street.

'Funny, really, first time I ever sat by myself.' She thought of Lena. Mysterious Lena, silent Lena, Lena that always promised, that cheered her up, that told her the fortune in a teacup, that laughed when she got drunk. The sudden tiny laugh in the long narrow room might have come from a fairy.

'Dear Lena. Always so cheery,' and at last looked up the room.

'You don't mind?'

'Mind what, dear?' asked the barman.

'Me just sitting here,' Mrs Kavanagh said. Laughing, he said, 'Not at all.' And her immediate 'Thank you' was grave.

'That's all right,' he said, then came down the room, stood there.

'You all right, dear?'

'I'm all right. Thank you. Nice of you to let me sit. I'm going now.' He leaned very close, 'Something on me?' he said. She shook her head, rose from the table, made an effort to smile.

'Thanks for letting me sit. Good morning.'

'Good morning, dear,' he replied, and watched her hurry into the road.

'Thought she was ill,' and he returned to his glasses, and watched the clock. It was a long road, and it did not matter to the woman that walked it. A friend seemed close to her ear, the words pouring in. A friend was close beside her.

'Do mind where you're going,' the lady said, towering, looking down.

'Sorry,' Mrs Kavanagh said, and went on. And talked and talked to herself.

'There always used to be something,' and Lena back, and she sighed for Lena. 'I hope nothing's happened to her. Course not. She'll be there waiting soon's I get in the door. Ah! We were all right, once.' When of a sudden she stopped dead and cried out, 'Get out of my way,' a passer-by stopped to stare, and then went on, and Mrs Kavanagh didn't even notice him, Mrs Laurent being so close to her that time, the one that didn't leave anybody alone, the one that could have talked to Mr Faulkner. The one that wished to see her home.

'I hate her. Never left me alone, not once.' She stared madly, anxiously, intensely into every passing face, but none was Lena.

'The first time ever that she didn't come. Oh God! If only she'd come last night. That bloody wind, that dark, the lights are always going out, and the bloody lifts are no different.' The thoughts confused, rocked her, made the road move, made her stop by the sandbin, wait, looking neither right nor left, but staring down, as though by some miracle the missing friend might rise out of the very ground.

'Nothing now.' Stopped again, walked on.

'Nothing.'

'She was quite right last night, I *was* tired, God, I was tired. I suppose those people are good sometimes.'

Would the road never end? She didn't know, she didn't care. She walked straight into the next pub, and this was crowded. She huddled in a corner. The man beside her, concerned, said, 'Get you something, Mrs?'

'Please. Thank you, sir.'

'There!' The road had suddenly ceased to move, the people vanished, she was in the corner, quiet under the noise, under the glitter. She tried to smile at the man, couldn't, she raised her glass.

'Thank you, sir,' she said.

'Welcome,' and the man forgot she was there, leaned close

to a friend and both wondered if April Blossom would come up in the three-thirty.

'I'm going now,' Mrs Kavanagh said, this time smiled, touched his hand. 'Very good of you.'

'Ta ta.'

And there was the road again, the never ending road. Already she could feel the approach of her tower, see the height of it, again thought of Lena, longed for Lena.

'Oh God! If anything's happened to her, oh no, oh no . . . !'

'Look out, woman.'

'*Sorry.*'

'Should bloody well think so, too.' She closed eyes, suddenly cried inside herself. 'Where am I?' She was on the road, she was walking, and the words were falling to the ground. And three more travelled all the way from the end of a long corridor, struck her in the ear.

'You are discharged.' Go. Good morning, goodbye. Done. Finished. And two more that rode swiftly behind three.

'Next case.'

So she knew where she was, near the end of a road that sometimes swayed, sometimes stood still. And suddenly, another known place, so she stopped, dead, the door open, the old area with the lights and the glasses and the glitter. A fugitive glance at a barmaid admiring her hair in a mirror, a stout fist grasping a glass. She turned away, she walked on. The pace slackened, it was like saying goodbye to another friend. 'Ah!' she said, 'Ah!' and there it was, the concrete home. She stood, she pondered, she wondered, moved towards the entrance to the building, stepped back, looked up again, then turned slowly round, surveyed the world. She lay bare between the two, cried to herself. 'Lena,' and hoped she'd be there. One step, and then another, and the thought between.

'Never wanted it, never asked for it.' She entered, glimpsed the lift, the light glimmering, thought of the buttons, doors that were massive, looked round, as she always did, someone might arrive, see her in, do the trick, send her skywards to the right floor.

'Ah well!' Entered the lift, closed the gates, faced the mystery of many buttons. And then a last-minute entrant.

'Hello.'

'Hello.' And up, and up, and the words spent.

'Nice morning.'

'Yes . . . it is,' and stepping out gingerly, looking round, listening, feeling for a key, yielding a sudden sigh, and then another walk, another corridor. Optimism unfurled like a flag, fluttered in imaginary air. 'Hope Lena's there,' thought of more certain days when she *was*, the smile, and the basket dangling in a thin hand, and the neck of a bottle protruding. It was if the door of her flat was itself smiling. And then the lifebelt, a sudden knowledge. 'Lena has a key, thank God,' and then took out her own, fumbled with it, with the lock, her hand shook, and then the key turned, and the name waiting, and calling it, 'Are *you* there, Lena?' Silence.

'Lena,' and louder, and a slow pushing in of the door. 'I'm back, dear.' She entered, looked round. No change, it was last night and the one before, and a trail of days, and 'the things' there. She sat down heavily. When she looked at the clock she knew it was late, and the reassuring words again. 'Lena always comes.' She got up, removed coat and hat, hung them behind the door, went to the fire, switched on, went to the window, looked out.

'She'll come,' Mrs Kavanagh said. Then slowly back to the bed, and lying there. She closed her eyes, waited, listened. No wind. Silence. The room warming, a lift actually working, the return of the light. The day's yield obliterated a morning wrack. She glanced up the room to a brightness of fire, and her spirit lightened. She put talons on hope, was content to wait.

*

Next door Lil and Eddy stared at each other, and thought of news that was too sudden, talked of the woman next door, wondered if now her ears had begun to burn.

'Can't, Lil, not really, honest, just couldn't,' Eddy said. Lil was real, and said abruptly, 'She'll have to know.'

'I know that. I'm not stupid.'

'Never said you were, dear.'

'Sorry.'

'I hate telling her,' Lil said.

'Yes, yes, of course, I don't know, the things that happen, the way they happen.' She sensed his drawing back, *knew*, snapped the reply.

'The way they *don't*.'

'So sudden,' Eddy said, 'you do have to think about these things, Lil. Can't we think it over?'

'No. You can't stand there just thinking about it. Mrs Biddulph was supposed to be *there*, waiting for her.'

'Blast them! Fancy them lifting her for *that*,' Eddy said.

'They just don't *like* this lifting business, Eddy. I'm tired *tell*ing you. Pity those damned supermarkets were ever invented.'

'What a world.'

'You won't then?' asked Lil, jumping to her feet.

'Told you. Daren't, couldn't face the old dear, telling her her friend wasn't coming.'

'Very well,' Lil said, and rushed from the room. '*I'll* do it,' and the door opened and slammed again, and Eddy sat quiet, and useless, and sad.

'Perhaps I should've really, yes, I should have gone and told her.' Then he heard another door bang, and knew Lil was in *there*. 'Lil's good any time,' a forced balm to his discomfort. 'Ah well! It's how it is.' He filled black moments with tea, the handy lifebelt, wondered how Mrs Kavanagh would take the news.

'And the very day they decided not to knock Kavanagh. Bastards. They just won't leave anybody alone,' and he returned to the sitting room, switched on the tele, watched 'Flower Pot Men'. He hoped Lil wouldn't be too long.

*

Lil paused on the threshold, felt for the key, opened the door, put a foot inside, called.

'You there, dear?' There was no answer and she went inside, saw the woman in the bed. Tiptoeing down the room, she called again. 'You asleep, Mrs Kavanagh?' She bent over the woman in the bed. 'Are you . . . ?' And saw her lying fully dressed on the bed. 'You all right?' There was no reply. She entered, silently closed the door, crept down the room, bent over her. 'You asleep?'

'Who's that?'

'Me.'

'*Who?*'

'Mrs Winten.'

'Oh!'

'*Do* open your eyes, dear. It's all right.' And opened them, stared up at the visitor, said, 'I'm tired today.'

'Been a long day,' Lil said. Mrs Kavanagh tried to sit up, reached out a hand, Lil took it.

'Course. It *is* you,' she said, and Lil sat down.

'You ought to be in bed, dear.'

'She didn't come,' Mrs Kavanagh said. All the way back today I was thinking, "she'll be there, the tea ready," it sort of carried me all the way home.'

'We are sorry,' Lil said.

'Mean,' Mrs Kavanagh said, 'I told him I wanted to go in.'

'Lie back,' Lil said, feeling for the words, knowing them, knowing they must come. The room felt it, the woman in the bed felt it, suddenly knew:

'She's not coming.'

'No, dear. She isn't.'

'Oh *no*. God! I was expecting her, she *always* comes,' and she turned her face to the wall, gave a low scream, 'don't tell me.'

But Lil leaned close to the Kavanagh ear, held both her hands. 'They picked her up in Soonan's.' The hands came free, clenched on a pillow. When the words came she no longer heard them.

'Can't tell you how sorry we are, dear. Quite upset Eddy, you know what he's like.' She didn't know, and she didn't care. 'Go away,' she said. Then awkwardly, in an awkward moment. 'Let me tidy you up,' Lil said.

'Go . . . *away*.' She turned over, threw wide her arms. 'Christ curse them,' covered her face, cried, 'Go away, leave me *alone*.' Lil sat on, stiff, still, listened, watched her rock in the bed.

'Only one I had.' And Lil said nothing.

'It doesn't matter now.' And Lil was dumb.

'Nothing,' Mrs Kavanagh said, 'nothing.' Lil rose, knew at once it should have been Eddy. He was good with things like that. She stroked the woman's hair, then her hand came down the arm's length, gripped the hand she found. 'There! There!' she said.

'Go away. Leave me alone.' It shattered Lil. 'I shan't be a sec, Mrs Kavanagh,' she said, hurried from the room thinking, 'Eddy'll know what to do, sure of it. Poor woman. Really shook me, just looking at her.'

Mrs Kavanagh heard the click of the door. She rose from

the bed, went slowly there, turned the key in the lock, put it in her pocket. She sat down at the table, folded her hands, thought how, on the other side, her friend should sit. And then she was very still, and the head had fallen a little forward. She stared about the room.

'Lena! Picked her up, pi . . .'

She got up and began a slow pacing of the room, and sometimes she would stop abruptly, pick up, and look fondly upon some object or other, 'her things'. A vase, a photograph, a work-basket, a button box, picked them up and held them, then put them down again. So backwards and forwards, a voyage down her days, and the things were still there, warm to the touch, known.

'Lena,' the voice thread-like, trembling, and so down to the fire, before which she now sat, hands clasped, nervous fingers pulling and pulling at what would never be there. And then a slow shaking of the head. She rose again, went slowly towards the window, drew the curtains, looked out, down. The curtains shook as the hands shook. There had once been a path, short, private, and it jutted out from the world, and when she walked to the end of it her friend was there, and she would turn and walk back and at the other end her friend was still there.

'Lena!' It had been like that. 'Lena,' she muttered again, 'I *expected* you, I did, I *did*,' and giving way again, 'nothing,' she said, 'nothing.' Once Lena had come to see her, found her kneeling in the middle of the room.

'Praying, dear?'

'Thinking,' she had replied. 'Just thinking.'

She wouldn't come now, nor tomorrow, nor the day after, nor the day after that. They get you, they always get you, and the teeth bared in a sudden, pointless, hopeless anger, and she cursed them again in the name of Christ.

'They could have let me *in*. They could have let Lena *go*.'

And heard the voice in the room, the footsteps, the laughs, the sitting down, the tea, and the flashes from the bottle, the world triumphant in the circumference of a room.

'Perhaps they'll let her off,' chasing the rainbow, 'she'd be back then.' Only perhaps. The sudden loud knocking on the door did not disturb her, nor the call of Mrs Winten, nor the voice of her husband, and she let them call and hammer on the door, delivered to herself the message. 'I don't care.'

And back to the window, and drawing the curtains again, and looking out and down, then she returned to the table and picked up the chair. She put it under the window, and for a while she sat in it, closed eyes, muttered softly to herself. Climbing on to the chair she slowly turned the catch, gave a slight push, felt a sharp breeze in her face, and when the window blew wide and clear of her grip, blessed herself with closed eyes, put her head out, pressed hard against what was solid behind her, threw out her arms, fell.

*

Falling, she cried, 'God!' and thought of Lena. Falling, she thought of footsteps that she would not hear, and Lena would never say 'hello!' And, still falling, the hurricane in the ears, the voices, the words, hammering home: Who are you, what is your name, and where do you live, how old are you, and show us this son of yours, in the flesh, and what is his real name, and why don't you just do what you're told to do, we know everything about you which means *everything*, and in spite of that we continue to ask the questions and watch you which it is our duty to do. Kavanagh then, a small woman that gets drunk, and in and out and in and out of the place where you go as regularly as the tick of the clock. And that *mystery* about you, and the daft look that so often goes with it whenever you are asked why you have come yet *again*.

And this endless voyage of yours to meet nice people as if you were the only one in the world that knew what nice people were, and this habit of yours of putting a whole pension down your throat, and the thing that grows *big*, and is yet the same, the hand on you, so being collected by the law in the self-same way. And this shaking hands with the whole world whenever you decide that the moment for hitting the bottle has at last arrived. And never attaching any importance to the words that are spoken to you. Exception is *not* the rule today, madam, and you know it. We say do this and do that, go here and go there, and you do not, and sometimes we say, 'wait', which is another duty to do, we say where were you *born* and you close your mouth like a trap. And *how* old is this son of yours, and what is the name of his ship that seems to be under way forever, the oceans voyaged, the world circled, yet this ship never arrives and is nameless. *We* think it is a dream, after which we ourselves are lost. And this friend of yours, this Lena Biddulph, who might, like you, be the world's friend, hidden and hugging yourselves together in a little house, in a littler street, and we have bent and we have striven yet there is still missing the fragment that will make the pattern of your lives, which, when found, will be nailed to a desk, after which you would always be known to us. There are those, and not by God appointed, that worry about the unanswered question, the thing that is not done. And this strange configuration of your mind that endows stupidity with the quality rightly belonging to common sense. Sense that is sheer, and no nonsense for miles. You appear to be made happy by the single act of being left alone, your erstwhile friend companion to it. Only another dream, madam, though in the world in which you live today, it has long been stone dead.

The State wishes to embrace you, and you will not accept it, the one grace upright in the day we live, the dream held until there is no further reason in it. You are discussed in big rooms and little rooms, and both your numbers are known, and when the orders have to be served, we serve them.

And this you'll recall, we did, some three years ago, we checked, and found that we had razed your home. London is full of relics of the grey time that was both long, and voiceless. After which we raised you to the sky, and though we admit that the height was terrific, we remembered nevertheless that you were there, since, from time to time, we sent a person your way to see if you were still upright. Yet others would write you from time to time, the usual reminder that we were still around, and would remain so until the day a name was erased from a book. Our virtues are shrouded in moral fervour, to which we attach a sickening faithfulness, duty being the one lifebelt that holds fast in the world about us today. Yes, and you may never believe this, but you were even noted walking home alone from a place where the words had been laid bare for you. Heard the window open, watched you climb, heard the crash of glass, and were even aware of the void that loomed up, and the rushing air that followed after. It is said that there was no sound save that of one that rushed down to find you, that gave another cry when she lifted you up and put you down again. And even she must have realized then how safe you were forever in the overcoat that you lived in.

Later, we were told that you cried in a public place when a gentleman informed you that you were free. One close to you at that moment said that the words were stones in your ears. After which, we understand, this person took you away to a quiet place and gave you tea, and even offered to accompany you back to your home, something that she had done on countless occasions. But again you said 'no', which is a word you used more often in your lifetime than the word 'yes'. So all your life you cried out to be left alone, and you are left so, and meet the full measure of the word closest to you.

As to this great friend of yours, we would say she is safe, a door closed, and the key now turned. Though we are not wholly certain of it, this friend of yours may herself founder. She was torn by the news, and by the act, though the thought that preceded it will ever remain a mystery to her, since there is now no door through which the secret could come out. And the words found by us in an old purse, were read, and understood, and accordingly you will go to a place called Willesden, and there will be no smoke. A name and a number are erased from a book.

One known to us as 'the digger', and to you by the name of Jenkins, will do the things that have to be done, since it is he that has the records and the facts of situations, and always alert and knowledgeable concerning them. So one will be sent to your home, there to examine the remaining fragments of your life, since as soon as one goes, another is waiting. Such fragments will be disposed of, and the wherewithal will go to your friend, Mrs Lena Biddulph, after which another will walk through your door for the first time. Some things are sad, and nothing whatever is simple.

And the words died in her ears.

*

One said, 'Easy there,' on a dark night, and another said, in a louder voice, 'Stand back there,' and they stood back, and watched, and were silent.

'Up, and easy, mate, *ea* . . .' whispered.

'Must have been mad.'

'Expect so.'

'Stand *back*,' so again they stood back, and then they saw what was lifted, and what slid noiselessly through a door, and what was large and white, purring on silent wheels, and after which a patch of ground was covered, and a voice said, 'Clear off now, it's all over,' and one by one they cleared off. Light from a torch staggered upwards, wavered, then held at a window that was wide to the sky.

Some three that had been very close to the moment ran wildly away, and more wildly down long semi-dark corridors, which was the world where they lived. Their mouths gaped, and the news was shouted through ever opening doors.

'Oh no.'

'Oh yes.'

'Poor old . . .'

'Awful,' and a door slam cut the voice in two. Others followed, like gunshots, and all was silent again. Behind one such, Lil was sick, and Eddy held her head, and the words were warm, comforting.

'There,' he said. 'There, Lil, dear. It's all right. You'll be all right in a minute,' and sat opposite her, the glass at his mouth, out of which he now sipped something that was always good in a mad moment. 'Ah!' and sat on the couch beside her. The mind wavered, the words knotted, then unknotted, he stroked her hair. 'The way things happen. Last thing I ever expected.' Two dead words followed after. 'It happened,' she said. When the room suddenly filled with a loud guffaw he got up and switched off the TV.

'Thought I'd switched off.'

'You hadn't,' she said.

'Lil.'

'What?'

'Doesn't matter,' he said.

'Might,' she said, 'might, Eddy,' clutched his fingers,

squeezed them, glad they were there, glad he was, closest to her in her whole life.

'You're a witness,' Eddy said.

'I know.'

'Feeling better, dear?' She gave a little smile, said nothing, and they sat still, in the still room.

'I won't sleep a wink,' Lil said.

'You will. I'll get a pill. Perhaps we ought to toddle now, dear,' and he helped her off the couch, put an arm round her, and they went to the door, and Eddy switched off the light.

'Be better in the morning,' he said, the final consolation.

IV

THE world was in the room, and she wasn't, being prone next door, very still, not bothering. Where the world sat the clock's tick was as heavy as feet. And twenty heads were as one, not moving. They watched, waited, saw a man make to rise, sit again, fumble with papers, and later, adjust his spectacles. Saw him finally rise, lean over, peer, read.

'If anything happens to me, Willesden, and no smoke.' The world heard a single guffaw.

'*Silence!*' This came, after which he again adjusted his spectacles, turned to his left, on which the helmet rose.

'Anything else?'

'Tenpenny pieces, sir, that's all.'

'Right,' and he sat down, and the spectacles were now firm on his nose. He folded hands, leaned across a table, peered again, searched, then saw her, and the authority that sat close beside her. The heads were quite still. Breathings waved down the silence.

'Mrs Lena Biddulph!' Who was still sat tight in her seat, and hands clenched.

'Get up,' authority said, and she got up. '*Go . . . up*.' She rose, went forward.

'Lena Biddulph?'

'That's my name.'

'Come forward, please,' and she came, abruptly halted.

'Closer, thank you,' and she went closer, watched the

hands, the spectacles. The hair was silvered, and thinning. He coughed. 'Ahem!'

'You *are* Mrs Lena Biddulph?'

'Am.'

'You were a friend of the deceased?'

'Was.'

'Can you tell me anything about her?'

'Nothing.'

'Why can't you tell me something about her?'

'Don't want to,' flung.

'*Why* don't you want to?'

'Too late.' He then drawled, and a slight sigh escaped him. He glared up at her.

'You would appear to have made up your mind, madam.'

'Have.' On which he sat back in his chair, folded hands on a lap, was suddenly casual. 'You were saying . . .?'

'Wasn't saying anything.'

'Ahem! You were, I gather, her closest friend?'

'Was.'

'You have seen her?'

'Have.'

'It is Brigid Kavanagh?'

'Was.'

'You lived together at one time?'

'Did.'

'Tell me about it, madam.'

'What for?' Then sharply, and authoritative. 'Where did you *live*?'

'Totall Point.'

'How long?'

'One week,' and after a pause, 'She stayed three years.'

'Where do you live now?'

'Wherever I happen to be at the time, sir.' A titter that flew.

'Silence please.'

'Go and sit down,' he said. She said nothing, and turned, walked quickly back to her seat, sat.

'You were positively *rude*,' authority said, but she said nothing. Lil was in the seat behind, and Eddy behind her, and now he leaned over, whispered in her ear, 'Let's get.'

'Ssh!' They listened, heard the words spoken, a foot scrape floor, a chair creak. They watched spectacles removed cased, and then an explosion of movement.

'Silence.'

'This case is adjourned until tomorrow morning at eleven o'clock.' A door wide, and an explosion of movement, a draught rushing in.

'Over,' Eddy said.

'Not *yet*.'

'For us, yes,' Eddy said. 'Finished. Done with.'

'Queer, wasn't it?'

'Ah!'

'She was a caution, wasn't she?'

Eddy said nothing, half pulled her down the room, they passed through the door, this closed, they were out in the world again.

'Did you see the eagle eye on her?'

'I did.' They paused at pavement edge, looked left and right, and Eddy said,

'What now?'

'Let's *go*.'

'Right. In here,' and he pushed her gently into The Horse and Groom, took a corner table, sat down.

'I liked Biddulph,' Lil said.

'So did I. What a caution.' A man came quietly out from behind red curtains, leaned over the counter, watched them, and said nothing.

'Stout, Eddy.'

'Port, dear,' he said. 'You deserve it. You were very good. Always be a pity you didn't know, at the time I mean.'

'One never does, really.' They heard a heavy movement, a heavier sigh, looked up, saw.

'Morning,' the big man said. Eddy ordered drinks, these were served, the big man walked away. They were alone, the whole pub theirs.

'Never be the same again to me, Eddy,' Lil said, drank. Eddy wiped his mouth, was prompt. 'What won't?'

'Next door.'

'Oh yes, for a sec I didn't know what you were at, Lil.' And a burst from Lil. 'I *was* sorry for Mrs Biddulph.'

'Can't be sorry for *everybody*, Lil.'

'You may be right.'

'Am,' and they touched glasses, 'Good health.'

'But *we're* here,' he said, pressed her hand, for the first time smiled. 'That's all that matters,' but Lil made no reply, stared into her glass, slowly sipped.

'D'you know what?'

'What?'

'I don't like it any more,' she said.

'*What?*'

'Where we *are*.' Eddy put down his glass, clapped a hand to his forehead.

'Don't *like* it?'

'No, I don't,' she said, rather fiercely, surprising him, and he wondered if she had a mood on, after the room, and something in it, and looking at it, and then the words.

'Where you are is where you're put,' he said. 'And that's it.'

'*Why* can't we?'

Flustered, he burst out with, 'How the hell do I know?'

'No need to lose your temper.'

'All so sudden, Lil, I mean not liking where we are. It was

all right before, and it's all right now.'

'Mrs Kavanagh was right,' Lil said.

'This *is* a turn-up,' he said. 'I thought you were happy.'

'It's the way I feel,' she said.

'Ah!' he said. 'Come on, let's go.' But she sat tight.

'Come *on*, some fresh air.'

'In a minute,' she said.

'This place is *empty*,' he said. 'Pity we didn't go to The Marquis.' Lil's hand shook, the drink spilt, 'there,' she said, '*there*?'

'What's the matter?'

'They were both there last week, and that Finch served them with flat beer just to get them out, that probation lot'd been in, *talked*. Say Finch was glad to get rid of them. Dirty, I call it.'

'It was for the best,' he said.

'Upset Mrs Kavanagh no end, like they'd cut off all the years she'd been going there with a sharp knife. She cried about it, and Mrs Finch tried to do her best.'

'What the hell's she going on about?' thought Eddy. 'We were all right yesterday. High up? What's that got to do with it? It's our *home*, where we live.'

'Lil.'

'Get me another drink,' she said.

He rose, picked up the glasses, 'Why can't we just go, Lil? *Now*?'

'Get me another,' and the voice hollow.

'All *right*.'

The big man gave him a smile and said, 'Right,' served him.

'Ta,' then slowly down the room, and thinking, 'It's knocked her, that's it, real knocked, poor Lil.'

'There,' he said, stiffly, sat again, wished her more good health, and Lil sipped away, and was silent. Inwards, Eddy growled. 'Should never have gone there, course she had to. So easily upset. No doubt she'll be rushing off to Holloway Friday to see the other one. Lil all over.'

'Lil?'

'Well?'

'I'm sorry,' he said. 'Should've known. Call it delayed shock, so I believe.'

'Wish we could be somewhere else.' Wish had become dream in a moment, and then he broke it.

'It is Friday, isn't it? I mean the Biddulph stuff?' Her angry glare surprised him, and he sat back in his chair.

'Well, it isn't Saturday,' she snapped. He lost control, shouted in her face, 'Should never have gone.'

'Had to. Talk sense,' she said.

He took both her hands, leaned in, said gently, 'You are good, Lil,' but she lowered her head, did not answer. So he thought this morning might become a mile long if they went on like this, and again nibbled at a wish, a hope. 'I'll go with you,' he said.

'Where?'

'To visit Mrs Biddulph.'

'What for?' Her reply was too abrupt, he didn't know.

'*Well?*'

'Thought you'd like me to, that's all.'

'Well I *don't*.' Suddenly he forgot the room where the woman lay, the man with the spectacles, the guffaw that had broken a silence, knew who he was, boss.

'Come *on*,' he said, and banged down his glass so hard Lil thought it would shatter. She finished her drink, got up.

'Right!' he said, took her arm, hurried her out of the pub.

'Dead place,' he growled, 'absolutely. Chap never even said good morning. Good job I was on nights,' he added, but Lil looked another way, appeared to forget he was there, close, her husband.

'You're not angry, Lil?'

'Just upset.' He hugged her, watched for a bus that would return them to the aerial cell. When it drew up he pushed her on, rushed up to the top deck, flung himself down, glared through the window.

'Really knocked her. Never seen her like it before. Never. Thought she'd cry in that room,' staring out, at nothing, at everything. The bus stopped, and Lil was already on the pavement when he got down. It uneased him when she looked, not at him, but into some great distance, as if in a flash he were a stranger to her.

'Lil!'

'Well?'

'Hope you'll be all right soon,' Eddy said. In three words she clouded him with doubt. 'You think so?' What a change. In a single morning. Never been like this before. Never. Wants to leave. *Go*. Our home. He made to speak, didn't, and she said, calmly, precisely, 'Hadn't we better go?'

'Course,' Eddy said, but suddenly the steps were uncertain, a road leading anywhere, everywhere.

'Where'll we go?' he asked himself, then savagely, hating her, 'I said where will we *go*?'

'Somewhere,' she said, went on, and he behind her.

He gripped her arm. 'We're arguing over her grave,' he said angrily.

'After it's over nobody cares. Saw it in a flash, Eddy.'

'Let's not say any more. Not another single word, Lil,' and his eyes searched her, begged, and she was perplexed by this.

'All right,' she said, so they went on, but he heard nothing, being for the first time that morning, back in yesterday.

It was the noise, the suddenness, her screaming, after the

quiet, going on down, finding her, then coming up again, tearing down the corridor, running to the door where he waited, and he could not see her face, hands covering it.

'There!' he said, 'there!' seeing it all again, hearing it.

'What, Eddy?' and she looked up at him.

'Nothing.' He had to bend low when for the third time she said, 'Eddy?'

'I'll be all right in a minute,' she said.

'Home soon,' he said, and they hurried on, seeing nothing, hearing nothing, and thought 'soon', grabbed at the relief from this, they would be back, *in*, the door shut, he and Lil together. And then a shout in her ear. 'It's all there is,' he said.

'You see what I mean,' Lil said.

Their feet rang out on concrete, steps echoing, they were at the fringe of the heights, walked in quickly, were dwarfed, went quickly to the lift. This worked, so they buzzed upwards, and Eddy was glad, feeling the warmth of a known place long before he reached it. A key in the lock, a door closed, a silence.

'Ah!' He flung himself down on the couch, stretched, threw wide his arms, sighed with relief. 'Need a bloody drink after all that, Lil.'

'Get me one,' she called from the kitchen.

'Can I do anything?'

'Nothing.'

'Ah! that's better,' he said, gulped at the drink. Glad it's over.' And it wasn't, and he knew this the moment he remembered her, Lena Biddulph.

'God! A real snarler if ever there was,' and he wondered what Lil thought of her, deep, secret, in her own mind. 'Rushing off to see her at Holloway, a perfect stranger. What for? It was all over, *finished*, their lives to live. Forget it, blot it out.'

He shut his eyes for a moment, then quickly opened them, just to realize a fact. 'Home. At last.'

'Ready,' Lil called, and he went into the kitchen and sat down.

'Good,' he said. 'Smells good.'

'Glad. You always do enjoy what I cook for you.'

'That's nice,' Eddy said.

'What?'

'*Smiling.*' They ate in silence.

'Lil!'

'What?'

'Oh . . . nothing.'

'Glad then.'

And he wasn't, as he ate, as he watched her, the day different, everything happening in a single morning. It was hearing a crack in the ice, seeing a ripple on the lake, a hand on their door, pushing it in, and a voice saying, 'Just heard. Let's know when you're off.' His knife and fork fell with a clatter, he stared at Lil.

'What's the matter, Eddy?'

'You know what.'

'I don't know what.'

'You do. Said it. Want to go, leave here, our home. Why? Count of something that's all over, finished. D'you *have* to see that one Friday?'

'Well really!' exclaimed Lil. 'Really!'

He rose, leaned across the table, delivered the ultimatum.

'Wasn't *she* happy then?'

'You *have* got a mood on.'

'So've you.'

'I thought you were sorry for her.'

'*I was.*'

'And Mrs Biddulph. What about her?'

'Asked for what she got.'

'Eat your dinner,' she said, handed back his knife and fork. The expression on her face bewildered him. He heaved it out, being afraid.

'You wouldn't leave *here*, Lil? There's nowhere else. It's *mad*.' Lil, calm as a lake, said, 'We'll see,' continued her meal, forgot him.

'You've upset me,' he said, 'upset me no end,' and he jumped up, rushed back to the sitting room, leaving Lil with thoughts that were real, solid, certain.

'Poor woman,' she thought. 'He doesn't even understand. Absolutely alone. Picking her up like that. What bloody next?' She got up, was resolved, knew the answer. She would go Friday. She found Eddy reclining on the couch, absorbed in his newspaper, and she didn't disturb him. She had been angry with him, not understanding, and then he looked up, smiled, 'There you are.' A softness in him touched her, got right home, so a sudden wish wavered, was beyond reach.

*

Eddy had finally said 'yes', then at the last moment, hedged. It was the wrong kind of ripple in the daily order of their lives, that had always been at fixed compass points, beyond which there seemed to him no reason ever to go. He was happy in his work, contented with the daily round. And so, he thought, was Lil.

He was sorry about Mrs Kavanagh, sorry about her friend. But there were limits. And he hated the idea of his wife rushing off to meet an old woman in prison. He longed for her to forget about it, leave it alone, all over, no longer any of their business. These things just happened, 'it's just the way things go', nothing special about the situation. They alighted from the bus, and the surroundings were new to him, though he noted with some relief that there was a pub on the corner.

'Come for company, Lil, that's all.'

'You won't come in?'

'*No.*' Laughing, she said, 'They won't bite you. These people are good in their way.'

'No.'

'*Why?*'

'Be . . . cause I . . . don't . . . want . . . to. That's all.'

'As you wish.'

'I'll be in there,' he said, pointing pubwards. 'I'll wait.'

She was suddenly angry, and he had never seen her look so angry. It aroused his own, and when the whisper came it was fierce, the grip on her arm, tight, strong. 'You know what it's all about?' he said. Her lips tightened, she didn't appear to know.

'It's about two old women burrowing into our lives, Lil. That's it.' She turned her back on him, walked away, and he watched her enter the building.

'This Mrs Laurent,' he said, scowling, 'who the hell's she?' He walked into the pub and sat down.

*

A cold draught struck Lil the moment she entered the building, and she felt strange, in a strange place. The corridor was empty. A man came out of a room, saw her staring about, came up to her.

'Yes?'

'Mrs Laurent's office,' she said.

'Of course. *That* way, madam, third on your left.'

'Thank you.'

Her pace slackened as she drew near the door, and when she reached it she did not knock, hearing voices in the room, and the conversation so clear the door might have been wide to the wall. She kept looking back, and a little afraid to knock.

'A ghastly mistake,' the voice said.

'A woman's voice,' thought Lil. 'Perhaps that's her.' And a man's voice. 'These things just happen.'

'They could have left her till the morning.' Lil put up a hand to knock, didn't.

'She wouldn't have run,' the woman said.

'In these matters you cannot always rule out enterprise,' he said.

'They could have left her a little longer, the fate of the country wasn't at stake,' and the tone much sharper. The reply stacatto, terse. 'But they didn't, *did* they?' The tone of voice indicated that he was already tiring of a known situation.

'She asked for it. We know that,' the woman's voice.

'Must be her,' thought Lil, the hand in air again.

'A pair of petty criminals. I knew them so long they were like members of my own family. Poor woman. She did so want to go back.'

'Faulkner probably thought he was right,' the man said. And a prompt reply, 'A lot of people do.' A sudden chortle. 'May have done the trick, really,' he said, as though Mrs Kavanagh, falling, had been practising on her one day off from the circus.

'Well . . .!'

'Yes. It is her,' Lil thought, and knocked.

'Somebody knocking, Mrs Laurent.'

'Come in.'

She entered the room, closed the door behind her, did not advance.

'Yes?' She stuttered. 'Sorry, didn't know you were engaged, madam. It's about Mrs Biddulph.'

'Do sit down.'

'Thanks.' On which the man hastily bundled papers under

his arm, rushed away, saying, 'See you,' and slammed the door after him.

'Well now. You want to visit her?'

'Yes. Promised her.'

'She'll be glad to see *anybody*.'

'I know.'

'She's difficult, and sometimes can be *very* difficult.'

'I understand,' Lil said.

'Sorry about your neighbour. Had you known her long?'

'Not long. Simply hello, good morning, that sort of thing,' Lil replied. Lil fidgeted, made to get up, sat down again, Mrs Laurent sensed urgency, said, 'I'll make the necessary arrangements, Mrs . . . er . . .'

'Winten,' Lil said. She hated the room, the woman in it. She thought of Eddy, waiting, watched the woman write out a note.

'There!'

Lil got up. 'Thank you.'

'Good morning.' Lil turned. 'What d'you suppose will happen?' The first smile came, the voice casual. 'Hard to say. But she's an old customer. Both were. Knew them for years,' she paused, then added in a sharper tone of voice, 'These supermarkets are a great temptation, Mrs Winten.'

'Suppose they are, really,' Lil replied.

'She was always afraid of the height,' Mrs Laurent said.

' 'Spect so. Never said anything to me ever, but then I rarely saw her, and she *did* like to mind her own business. Sometimes you wouldn't know if she was in or out. Kept to herself mostly.'

'Rather fond of her glass.'

'Know that. Perhaps there wasn't anything else,' Lil said.

'You could be right.'

'*Looked* lonely, but you couldn't say anything, sort of distant she was.'

'They had their own kind of happiness,' said Mrs Laurent.

'Suppose so.'

'They were *very* close.' Mrs Laurent rose and led her visitor to the door.

'One of the nice things about them,' she said. 'And now,' she continued, emitting a sigh, 'and now, if you'll excuse me . . . She'll be glad of a visitor,' on which Lil swung round on her.

'You *said* that.' She was glad to be out of it, free of the room, and the woman in it, glad to reach the end of the corridor. She hurried across the road to where Eddy was waiting.

'Here I am.'

'Good. How'd it go?'

She thought suddenly, 'Perhaps Eddy's right, perhaps I shouldn't have, mind my own business,' and a restlessness grew, she wanted to go home.

'I said how'd you make out?'

'All right. Seeing her three o'clock Friday,' and a later thought dragged, a sudden ache to justify, 'Promised to go, said I would. *Must*.'

'Miles away,' he said, and pulled out a chair. 'Here. Sit down.' She sat on the chair edge, uncomfortably.

'Get easy, Lil, get *easy*,' he said, and turned for the counter.

'Nothing for me.'

He threw the reply over his shoulder. 'As you wish,' and then sat down again. He finished his drink, and they left the pub. Arm in arm they dawdled their way down the road. He looked anxiously at her.

'You all right?'

'Yes.'

'What's she like?'

‘Who?’

‘Probation lot?’

‘All right, I suppose.’ Lil had become monosyllabic. He halted, said quite seriously, ‘One hour there Friday then, and no longer,’ and she did not reply.

‘Lil!’

‘Stop fussing.’

‘This Friday,’ he said, ‘and that’s all.’

This came.

V

SHE had seen her on two, sometimes three evenings a week when she arrived at the Kavanagh flat, and inevitably carrying a bag from which the neck of a bottle usually protruded. Tall, thin, a woman in her sixties, she imagined, that passed in and out of the block as secretly and silently as her friend. A set routine, broken only by the occasional contingency, carrying the same bag, wearing the same coat and hat. Now they had got her again, and for the self-same reason, a nature that turned greedy the moment it entered a shop. She spoke to none. So, too suddenly, she was close to one that she did not know, no more than she knew or understood the small woman that lived next door to her. And she thought of Mrs Biddulph now, as the bus carried her to her destination. Perhaps they were mysteries, even to themselves. She alighted, and slowly approached the entrance, and rang the bell. Entering she was soon made aware of the machinery that worked within. The general clatter, the occasional rattling of keys, echoing footsteps, the continuous coming and going of visitors, an occasional fugitive call.

'Mrs Biddulph,' Lil said, 'Mrs Lena Biddulph.'

'This way. Anything in your bag?'

'I haven't got a bag.' And was led to the long, narrow room, in silence, the door opened.

'Right.'

'Thank you.'

She saw the tables, and counted them, looked earnestly round, and finally saw her, approached gingerly, shyly, and still in her ears the loud clatter and the footsteps and the keys, and the waves of low murmurings that met her as she entered.

'Mrs Biddulph?' She was seated alone at the table, the head bent forward, the clenched fists resting nervously at the table's edge, and she did not look up when addressed.

'I came, dear,' Lil said, and sat down opposite her. She did not see the others, only the one that still remained silent and, judging from her very pose, indifferent. So for the third time she prompted. 'I promised, and I came.'

Lil was suddenly aware of the clock, and its giant tick, and of the tall woman that stood beneath it. She returned the stare. Mrs Biddulph finally elected to look up, and remarked casually, 'So I see. Thanks.'

'How are you?'

'How'd I look. Forgotten your name.'

'Lil Winten. I'm next door to your friend.'

'What happened?'

'Doesn't matter now,' replied Lil, 'all over, really.'

'Know.'

'Pity.'

'Bastards.'

Lil leaned across to the woman, gave a little smile, was in a moment serious. 'Sorry they got you,' she said, again found herself staring at the clenched fists. Would they ever loosen, relax?

'Know why she did it?'

Flustered, Lil said, 'Who?'

'Brigid. Mrs Kavanagh. My friend.'

'No, I don't.'

'Someone told her I'd been lifted. Swine. That, and the other thing.'

'The other thing' sent Lil into the clouds.

'Oh, I see. Understood, dear.'

Mrs Biddulph seemed closer still. 'Do you. Really? Fancy that.'

'What'll you get, d'you think?' asked Lil.

'Ditto if they say yes.'

Lil's whisper was a real effort. 'I *am* sorry.'

'So'm I. Told you.' The chuckle shocked Lil. She sat well back in the chair.

'Come again?'

'Course.'

'Thank you,' replied Mrs Biddulph. Lil appeared to be seeing this woman for the first time, real, lost in a room. 'Course I will.' The air was lighter the moment Mrs Biddulph smiled.

'You're a nice girl,' she said.

'Lena?'

'What?'

'When did you first meet Mrs Kavanagh?'

'Oh dear!' And Mrs Biddulph sat back, suddenly laughed, the clenched fists came apart, and she stroked her lips with the fingers of one hand, laughed again.

'In the gutter. Twelve o'clock, remember that to this very minute. I was on my way home. She was flat out. Took her home.'

'Ill?'

'Drunk.'

'When was that?' and knew she was talking, for talking's sake.

'Doesn't matter. Nothing matters after it's happened.' The chuckle again, and now followed by a Biddulph hand that suddenly covered the visitor's. 'Every time she left the house the brewery shares went up. Fact.' And she laughed again, and Lil didn't.

'Just like that?'

'Like that, dear.'

'How old was she, Lena?'

'When I come on her, around seventy, I'd say, always told that lot she was sixty, fair codded them.'

'Who, dear?'

'Where the helmets live. I once had a place of my own, little house, end in a terrace, took her home.'

'And her son?'

'That's where he was born,' Mrs Biddulph said.

'I don't understand, Lena, at that age . . . I mean . . .'

A slight titter, and then, 'Her son was born in Gag Lane, dear.'

'Never knew she had a son,' said Lil.

'Ah, but she did, told you, and he came right out of the tealeaves, as you might say. Born in the teacup.'

So she was back in Gag Lane, and the light gone, but the fire supplied all, and the warmth, as they sat close together at the table. And she remembered the night, and the tea, and the bottle, and that they were happy. In a whole day they had kept out of the world's way, and were content.

'There's a stranger in your cup, Brigid.'

'*No* . . .'

'Yes. A tall young man, dark, see him as clear as the day, dear, he's wearing a blue suit, and a jersey with it. Might be a sailor. Lots of hair, very black it is.' When Mrs Biddulph looked up she saw her visitor wide-eyed, and gave her a little smile.

'How it was, dear. Poor woman. She believed everything I said. Before you could say knife he was real to her. *Real.* Think of that then. And whenever the light came into her head he was there, real again.'

'Light?'

'When she was drunk, Mrs Winten, I mean drunk. Funny, but every time she got drunk he was more and more real to her. Strange, isn't it? Talk about hanging on to something alive for her ever after. Made her happy. What's wrong with that?'

And Lil said, 'Nothing, oh nothing.'

'Ah! I'm sorry she's gone, I'll miss the laughing most of all.'

'I'm sure you will,' replied Lil.

'I *mean* that.'

'I know you do, Lena.' Mrs Biddulph rose, leaned over, and Lil felt the hot breath in her ear, received the conspiratorial words.

'And then she started writing to him. Think of that. Shows you, doesn't it? Believed in him. *Real*. That bitch Laurent who had me lifted, I heard her say to somebody that Brigid was mad. Fancy that. Silly cow.'

Lil couldn't hold back the smile. 'Not really?' she said.

'Did.'

'How very extraordinary.'

'Ah! Wrote to him whenever she was tight. Flesh and blood now, told you,' rose again, bent over the visitor, said breathlessly, 'real.'

'How strange,' Lil said, 'rather sad though.'

'Told me one night, "He *is* a sailor. *Seen* him." Even told me the name of his ship,' and after a long pause, said quietly, 'I thought there was something lovely about it myself. Never stopped talking about this man from the tealeaves. You'd have to be there just to believe it. Way she hung onto him, never let go. Sometimes she'd be so drunk she couldn't hold a pen, so then I'd write the letter for her. But of course she had to be well away before I did that. And the things she used to tell him.'

And once again Lil said, 'How extraordinary.'

'Was. At the time, dear. The fuss she'd make about writing to him once a week. I never breathed his name myself, only when she got into her cups. Flesh and blood to her then, and once she told me she'd seen him in the room. Sometimes I would see her standing behind the curtains, a shaky finger pulling on them, her looking out, as if in a sudden moment her sailor son might come walking down the lane. But if we were both drunk then we just waited until the next time. Even told me the name of his ship one night. *Devonian*, she said. Now how'd a name like that get into Brigid's head? Often asked myself that. Once she said to me in dead earnest, "I mustn't miss the post Wednesday, Lena, mustn't." So important to her it was. So I said to her where is this ship? Caught her out then. Left her dumb. But I wouldn't crack her sweet dream on the poor woman, not me, so I told her one Wednesday, "It'll be one of them M.V. boats. Better address it care of the General Post Office," and that's what she did. Laurent posted three for her once, so she said.'

'Did *you* ever post any?'

And Mrs Biddulph gave another slight titter. 'Course not. Where'd I post it to? Dreamland? I'd tell her yes, okay, I'd send it off for her, go outside, crush it in my pocket, and come in again, then when she wasn't looking I'd chuck it into an old cardboard box right back of the cupboard. God! She used to worry me *real* sometimes. I mean the things she'd say. "It's strange Sean hasn't written, Lena," and I'd say "Perhaps his ship's just left port, in which case they'll send the letter on to him, the ship's agents I mean." I told her the General Post Office always knew the right port in the end. Reassured her that did. Whole thing just grew and grew, wouldn't believe it, but it did, and then he was really living inside her, and you couldn't ever get him out either. *Too* real, you see. She started going off to the Post Office on her own, making all kinds of inquiries, and once she wrote to two steamship companies inquiring about this son midwifed in a teacup. Used to laugh about it now and again, then suddenly I didn't laugh any more. Couldn't. Man at the Post Office was nice, he understood, told me about it, always a smile for her, and a slow shake of the head, and I can hear his "Sorry, Mrs Kavanagh, nothing today, but perhaps a letter *next* Wednesday." We'd collect the stuff from the State then and go off to The Marquis. Mr Finch, that's the man runs it, he was nice, specially if we both got tight and his missus'd see us home. We used to like just sitting there with a glass, listening to the talking and the laughing. Better than a lot of things I wouldn't talk about. Ah! When I think of it now,' and the Biddulph head suddenly shot up, the expression on her face quite changed, and seeming to alter the atmosphere of the room itself, a smile, suddenly home.

'Nice talking about it, remembering, I mean, makes her seem here sort of thing. Once she even thought he'd died on her, terrible it was, got it right on the brain one night. Cried. The way she cried. It made everything seem even more real than it was. I remember once when it was like that I suddenly wanted to laugh real loud, but I didn't, dared not in the end. Slept *together* that night. Had to.'

'How strange,' Lil said, herself in dreamland.

'Was, and it wasn't.'

Every head turned the moment she clapped her hands together.

'Christ! Can't believe she's gone, she has, hasn't she? I mean it *is* true? *I'm* not dreaming.'

'How pathetic,' Lil thought. 'No dear, you're not dreaming.'

'We had our duty to mind, and we minded it, and that's why we never got in anybody's way. Never. You're safe then. Once a month, first Thursday in every, we'd call to see God . . .'

'God?'

'That's it. Council lot. Real name was George but we called him George God, and the name stuck. Funny chap he was, really. Height of the dustbin, and such a stuck out chest, always wore a collar and tie, blue suit, sat behind a desk bigger than himself, and the room was *so* long, used to make us feel tired moment we come in the bloody door. Call your name out. You went. Once I thought I'd never reach the end of that damn room, damp's a wet sock. Always a little queue there, always somebody waiting. He used to have a special grin for a long queue, liking it better. So your turn came, so you went on down. Usual stuff. Name, number et-bloody-cetra, what were you doing now, were you all right, haven't seen you about lately, all that cod stuff. Some of it was so damned silly all you wanted to do was spit on your way out. Some of them crackpots actually think they own you.'

'I suppose so,' said Lil, dragging the words, still caught up in the dream, and staring at everybody in the room except the woman opposite her. After which there was a silence, the Biddulph lips set tight, and her own trembling words refusing to come. When she glanced at the clock Mrs Biddulph was quick to notice it.

'All do that,' the words like gunshots.

'What dear?'

'Can't get away fast enough some of them,' took a close look at her visitor, dropped her voice, asked, 'I know, dear. How it is. Know you're uncomfortable. It's the smell, isn't it?' Lil's reply was forced, she shook her head, wanted to smile, and didn't.

'It's not that at all.'

'Glad.'

'I'll have to be going soon.'

'Go then.'

'Not quite time yet,' Lil said. 'When will you actually know, dear?'

'When that lot makes up its mind. Not before.'

'You're not London yourself then?'

'Leeds. *Why?*'

'Just wondered. Any family, Lena?'

'Son. Daughter. Grown up. Got the message one day. One look said it. *Go*. Went,' and she flicked finger and thumb. 'Just like that. Beat it. Way it goes, dear. Anyhow, I was tired treading my heels up there.' A hallucinatory thread snapped, and Lil was clear of the dream.

'I'll come and see you again next week, Lena,' she said.

'Only if you want to.' And too abruptly, 'That *smell*,' Lil said. And Mrs Biddulph flattened the horror. 'Same as yesterday, you get used to a thing, dear.'

'So you don't know what you'll do when you get out?'

'Matter entirely for his lordship,' thrown off.

'I see.'

'Glad you do.'

'Won't keep you forever,' Lil said, laughed, 'only a bottle of gin.'

'Had a dream last night. Hate dreaming.' Lil turned away, looked down the room, at the others, the clock, listened to the murmurs. It made her think of church, quiet praying

'Poor creature,' she thought. 'Lena?'

'What?'

'How old are you, dear?'

Mrs Biddulph sat up, stiffened, cast a fierce eye at Lil. 'That's *rude*.'

'Course it was. And I'm sorry.' She wanted to take the woman's hands, press them, make her *feel* her thoughts, in the long room with the watcher watching. She saw Mrs Biddulph lie back, stare at the ceiling, then close her eyes. The fingers twiddled, were as suddenly clenched again.

'Always asked *her* that,' Mrs Biddulph said, head back, still with closed eyes. 'Whenever they got her, I mean.' And Lil was miles away when the eyes opened. She leaned forward

'Course you daren't, really, not there. I didn't much like some people that brought children with them. Awful when it was time to go, crying that went on.'

'Their own fault if they were there though,' Eddy said. She sighed. 'I suppose so.' She looked round the room, looked at Eddy, glad he was there, glad she was home.

'Lil?'

'What?'

'D'you *have* to go there again?'

'Don't *have* to, but I'm going.'

'Isn't once enough? She's a complete stranger to you.' The sharp tone of her voice surprised him, he pushed away the tray.

'She was till I got there, and then she wasn't, and then I knew what it meant.'

'What d'you mean?'

'You wouldn't understand,' she said. Suddenly irritated he cried out, 'How the hell d'you know that?'

'I know.' He was standing over her, a hand on her shoulder. She wondered what was coming.

'It's *over*,' Eddy said. 'It was *sad*, *at* the time. What about *us*, Lil?'

'What about us?' she asked, her voice calm. On which he rushed from the room, shouted, 'I'm kipping,' and slammed the door after him.

Only when she heard this did she get up and sit on the couch. She sat very still, she wanted to relax, and could only think of Holloway.

'I must. I *will*.' She remembered the Biddulph laugh, the titter, the single croak in the voice, involuntarily rose, went to the window, looked out, down.

'Funny really,' she thought, 'if it hadn't happened I'd never have noticed,' and she turned quickly from the window. Eddy was restless where he lay, turning this way man at a bus stop, just because she was happy doing it. Fact. Think of *that.*'

'I am,' Lil said, and didn't.

'Can't believe it, really. She never harmed a fly. Set people off laughing, but that's a good thing any time,' and she leaned once more towards her visitor, and whispered, slowly, 'No little garden path to her soul, dear. None.'

'Yes,' replied Lil, lost and bewildered in a flood of words, and noticing how suddenly relaxed Mrs Biddulph had become, the fingers no longer restless, the puckered brow gone. And Lil felt it and was relieved.

'You were saying, Lena . . .' and Mrs Biddulph immediately announced that she wasn't.

'Pity they didn't leave you together in Gag Lane.'

'Ah! They just said get and we got, but I wasn't having any bloody life in the sky, not for anybody, so I just kipped around after that. But she decided to go there. Always surprised me that. Lucky I myself wasn't all that far away from the Totall lot. Managed to see her when I could. If she happened to be "in", and I wasn't, then I'd look after her place for her, ditto when she was out and *I* was in. Understood each other, Brigid and me. She knew nobody *there*, just nobody, 'cept yourself, dear. Once talked about you to me. And then after all the damned fuss about razing Gag Lane to the ground, they didn't, standing up after all, ransacked of course, still are, stupid bastards they were. Ah! Even in Gag Lane you never knew where you were, one day to another. Never felt your front door was *really* tight shut, always someone around, spying, lot of it goes on, but I expect you know that, dear. Way it goes.'

Lil didn't know, but nevertheless nodded a reply, just for the occasion. She felt calmer now, after the deluge. The words that reached her from an old woman's mouth finally touched, and she was glad they had come

'And *I'll* think about all that,' Mrs Biddulph said, 'even after you've gone.'

'Do call me Lil.'

'Lil.'

'Nice. I like that.' The clock struck, stabbed the room, and Lil looked up as the heads moved.

'That's it then.'

'Looks like it,' said Lil. Some children cried, and a voice at the top of the room cried, too.

'It *is* time.' Mrs Biddulph rose, Lil followed, held the woman's arm.

'Anything at all I can bring in for you?' she asked. The final titter of the afternoon followed, and Mrs Biddulph shook hands with her visitor, bestowed the final smile.

'You couldn't bring in what I like,' she said.

'What's that?' asked Lil.

'The *stuff*.'

'Oh!' The root and anchor of a life that still bewildered Lil.

'I'll bring you *something*,' she said.

'Lena, dear,' Lena said.

'Lena.'

'Ta.'

'Goodbye now.' Mrs Biddulph took the proffered hand, shook it, half turned, said 'goodbye', and the next moment she had filed out of the room, and Lil went off with the other visitors. It was with a sigh of relief that she passed through the gate, though she still remembered the hand that lay in her own, remembered the smells.

'Awful place.' She stood, idly watched the traffic whizz by.

'Glad I went. Poor old thing. If I hadn't, I'm sure nobody else would have done.' She walked casually down to the bus stop, mingled with the others, then suddenly felt herself being stared at, looked, received the other's glance, and this said, 'one of us'.

'Never dreamed I'd be visiting a prison to see a complete stranger, never. If Eddy'd gone he would have understood.' And the bus jolted her home, and Eddy was waiting for her at the open door. Eddy, who liked doing things, had already made the tea, and now rushed away to bring it in.

'How'd you get on, Lil?'

'All right.' She stirred her tea, nibbled the bread, and Eddy sat and watched her.

'Sleep all right, Eddy?'

'Yes,' and he, too, sipped his tea, looked fondly at her over the cup's rim. 'I thought about it after you'd gone, Lil.'

'About what?'

'What you gone and done. Nice of you to go there, real decent.'

'Thanks for that. Glad I did. All on her own, poor dear. See her now, sitting all by herself if I hadn't gone.'

'Many there?'

'*Too* many. Packed.' The smells still lay in her nostrils, but she refused to mention them.

'I'll say they are,' he said, casually, then poured her another cup of tea.

'It's a strange world,' she said.

' 'Spect it is. What can you expect then? Times we live in now, can't do anything much, well, can you?'

'Eddy?'

'What?'

'I've a jolly good mind to go to the pictures tonight.'

'More tea?'

'No.'

'Why not then, Lil? Change'll do you good. Wish I wasn't on nights, go with you.'

'Some of the things she said made me want to laugh,' Lil said.

'Did they?'

'Course you daren't, really, not there. I didn't much like some people that brought children with them. Awful when it was time to go, crying that went on.'

'Their own fault if they were there though,' Eddy said. She sighed. 'I suppose so.' She looked round the room, looked at Eddy, glad he was there, glad she was home.

'Lil?'

'What?'

'D'you *have* to go there again?'

'Don't *have* to, but I'm going.'

'Isn't once enough? She's a complete stranger to you.' The sharp tone of her voice surprised him, he pushed away the tray.

'She was till I got there, and then she wasn't, and then I knew what it meant.'

'What d'you mean?'

'You wouldn't understand,' she said. Suddenly irritated he cried out, 'How the hell d'you know that?'

'I know.' He was standing over her, a hand on her shoulder. She wondered what was coming.

'It's *over*,' Eddy said. 'It was *sad*, *at* the time. What about *us*, Lil?'

'What about us?' she asked, her voice calm. On which he rushed from the room, shouted, 'I'm kipping,' and slammed the door after him.

Only when she heard this did she get up and sit on the couch. She sat very still, she wanted to relax, and could only think of Holloway.

'I must. I *will*.' She remembered the Biddulph laugh, the titter, the single croak in the voice, involuntarily rose, went to the window, looked out, down.

'Funny really,' she thought, 'if it hadn't happened I'd never have noticed,' and she turned quickly from the window. Eddy was restless where he lay, turning this way and that, sitting up, lying down again, remember his wife at the window, staring, staring, his rushing at her, saying 'don't', pulling her violently down the room. Lil jumped when the door burst open.

'*Can't* kip,' he said, and flung himself down beside her.

'What on *earth's* the matter with you, Eddy?'

'Wish to Christ I knew,' and when he looked at her realized she was looking everywhere but at him, and remembered a morning restlessness that had bewildered and frightened him.

'Lil?'

'Well?' His manner was strange, and she had never seen him looking so worried. 'What's the matter, Eddy?'

'You wouldn't?' he said.

'Wouldn't *what*?'

'Never mind.' She leaned against his shoulder, and then she listened to the stutters.

'We're happy here, Lil, it's our *home*, isn't it, I mean . . .'

'What *do* you mean?' He clapped hands to his face, exclaimed 'ah!' then turned his back on her.

'You think of nobody but yourself,' Lil said. The words were muffled through fingers.

'You don't *understand*.'

'Don't want to,' her voice rising. 'Leave me alone, Eddy.'

'Shock's still with you,' he said, 'that's it. Why'd it all happen anyhow?' a sudden aggressiveness in the voice.

He clasped his knees, rocked gently to and fro, stared at the carpet, wanting to say something, something sensible, something final, wanting to get close again, but only heard her footsteps as she ran down the road, and the sudden shout.

'Lil?'

'What now, Eddy?'

'Why couldn't we go to Kent for the weekend? Why? I rang Betty, and it's okay. She understood at once. We *both* want a break. I've hated these last two days, really have,' and looked at her, appealing, wondering, waiting, but Lil sat quite still, and said nothing. He longed to go, anywhere, just away, wanted it, *now*.

'Horrible for you,' he said.

'You're not usually like this, Eddy,' Lil said, ran her fingers down his arm.

'And you're not usually like *that*,' he snapped, 'and I'm on at half seven.'

'Yes, dear, I do know that,' Lil said, and the words lighter than the air they drifted on. She put arms round him, smiled, 'All right then.'

'Good.'

'I'm only being sorry for somebody,' she said.

'Know that already.' When she got up he followed. 'Let's go out.' She went to the bedroom, brought back his coat and cap.

'Where'll we go, Eddy?'

'*Anywhere*.' They came out together, and she paused at the door. 'Where then?'

'Far's the river and back again,' stressing it, if only to make it conclusive.

'It's cold out,' she said. He held her hand, they stood in the corridor, he looking up and down, again asking himself the question, 'What is wrong? What's happening to *us*? It's where we live, home.' They walked to the lift in silence, descended, rushed into the fresh air, left the towering mass behind them.

'Lil!' And he stopped dead.

'That's *enough*.'

And they went on. A warmth rose in him. 'Not me, dear, *you*.'

'That's *enough*.'

'Right. Here we go then,' and he waved down the first bus. They were silent on it, and silent off it. They hurriedly crossed the road.

'There,' he said, leaned on the wall, watched the barges go by.

' 'Tis chilly,' she said, and she leaned, too. A very important tug tooted, went on its important business.

'Always something happening down here, Lil,' he said, a cheer in the voice at last, and she was glad.

'Good to get away from the damned place,' he thought, turned, faced her, 'Well, isn't it?'

'Course it is.' Kent gnawed at him, he thought of it in terms of a whole county embracing her, even heard Betty calling to them from a top window. 'Hello, you two.'

'I could fix it with Fred Turner, Lil, get the weekend free.' And he waited for the answer.

'You know right well the inquest isn't over yet, and I've got to go.'

'Ah!' And suddenly, the lifebelt, the voice behind him, high, shrill.

'Lil. Good Lord. Fancy bumping into you,' and Lil turned, and cried.

'Why, it's Ann. Well, well. Small world.' He watched them embrace. He did not know the woman, wondered who she was.

'This is my husband, Ann,' cried Lil, 'Eddy. Ann Wakeham. I used to go to school with her, didn't I, Ann?'

Ann laughed, and Eddy said, 'How do you do, Ann,' though rather gravely.

'Let's go somewhere, Eddy,' said Lil, linked arms with him, with her friend, 'let's go.' They walked briskly down the embankment. Lil knew Eddy's direction, said quickly, 'I'd rather a cup of tea in a café, Eddy.'

'Okay.' He offered Ann a smile. 'Not every day you meet an old school friend.'

'Think of it, dear. After *all* these years,' Lil said. A babble of conversation struck Eddy's ears, ricochetted off into damp air.

'Here we are,' he said, and they entered an ABC, found a table, sat down, and he ordered tea for three. They ignored him, and he was glad of that. The tea came, and Ann served.

'Cake, Eddy,' asked Lil.

'Nothing for me. Thanks. Just the tea.'

'Ann?'

'Ta.'

The bursts of exchange confused Eddy, and the whisperings even more. He was astonished and happy to note the gayness in Lil's voice. It was like old times, before the world of old women appeared on the horizon.

'Ann's teaching now, Eddy,' Lil cried. 'Fancy that,' and turned with another big smile to her old friend. 'But you were always clever, Ann.' Ann blushed, and asked for another cake, and Eddy handed her this without a word.

'How long you been married, Lil?'

'Not all that long, have we, Eddy?' He wanted to say 'long enough', but didn't and gave them both a morning smile.

'You *must* come and see us,' Lil said.

'Of course,' Ann said, and then a special smile for Eddy, who promptly vanished behind his teacup. 'Where are you now then?'

'Totall Point. And you?'

'Edgware.'

'Fancy. Edgware,' said Lil. 'We are coming on.'

'Just getting away from the bloody place's done her good,' thought Eddy. She was so odd that day I thought I'd have to climb right into her head to get the answer.

'More tea, anybody?'

'No thanks.'

'I've had enough,' Eddy said.

'Totall Point,' mused Ann, and then abruptly, 'of course. Read about that in the paper.'

'We don't want to discuss that now, do we, Eddy?' When she looked at him she got the answer.

'Happening every day of the week,' he said, and Ann, catching his glance, got up, knew he wanted to be off.

'Well, it's been nice seeing you, dear, and I'll remember your kind invitation,' flung Eddy another smile, and left the table. The two women walked off, talking animatedly, leaving Eddy to do the usual. As he left the waitress gave him a wink, thanked him for the tip, and rushed away.

'Probably me,' he thought, 'got the whole bloody thing on the brain.' He joined them outside, and found them exchanging addresses.

'He'll be on day work in a fortnight, won't you, Eddy?' Forcing a smile, Eddy said yes, he would be. 'What about it?'

'Ann's coming to see us, dear, of course she is, aren't you, Ann?'

'Yes indeed.'

'We must be off, Miss . . .' Eddy said, linked Lil's arm in his own. She slapped his arm. 'Ann Wakeham, Eddy. You *are* a one. Forgetting already.'

'Sorry,' he said, and looked shyly across at his wife's school friend, such an excited person, so well dressed. 'Well goodbye, nice to have met you, Miss Wakeham,' and he shook hands, Lil following, and she gave her a violent kiss, 'and don't forget, dear, just drop's a card, and the rest's your uncle, isn't it, Eddy?'

'Course.'

Standing close together, they watched Ann go, waved her into the distance.

*

'Just fancy that,' said Lil.

Hugging her, he said, 'Nice surprise for you. Glad we came out. Tea was nice, wasn't it?'

'Lovely.' She tightened her grip on his arm, waited for the bus.

'Let's not bother,' he said, 'let's walk back. Nice girl, your friend, I mean. Bit on the posh side, isn't she?'

'Not all that posh, you *do* get some odd ideas into that head of yours,' Lil said.

'Do I, really,' and he laughed, held her at arm's length, 'you're better than her any time.'

'Come on. Let's get home.' She paused a moment at the playground, watched the children, and Eddy gave a pull on her arm, 'Come on,' and immediately waved down the first bus. And seated beside her he was suddenly miles away from the things that were real. Head against the window, he watched the world rush by.

'Lil.'

'Not another word,' she said.

She was yet close to Ann, a part of her life suddenly descended out of the blue, warmth in the surprise of it, the thought of her friend actually teaching. And living in Edgware, too. Imagine that! Can never get away from where you are, who you are, how it is, that's all. He's right. Stay where you're put. Ah well! She turned quickly. 'Eddy!' He, staring right ahead said, 'What?'

'You won't mind her coming, will you, just for the night.'

'Course not. What made you think I might?' She gave a quick toss of the head, 'Just came into my head, Eddy.'

'No *need*. Glad you met up again. *What* a surprise! Way you used to talk about her one time.'

'She's clever,' Lil said.

'Suppose she is.'

'She's nice,' Lil said. 'Not everybody is these days.'

'Telling me.' She looked fondly at him. Always the same, he'd never change, and she was glad of that. He was good, loyal, worked hard, did his very best. What more could you expect?

'Glad you liked her.'

'Made a change, these last few bloody days . . .' She clapped a hand on his mouth. 'That's enough.'

'Watching the tele all the time,' Eddy said, 'struck me it makes some people not want to do other things. I mean, you get into the habit of not wanting to do things. Ever noticed?' She laughed, and was touched by this. There was a simplicity in Eddy, and she respected it.

'Call ourselves lucky then,' Lil said.

'Lucky,' he said, and the bus pulled up with a screech.

'Here we are. *Back*.' They paused outside the block.

'Have I ever complained about what I am, where we are, have I?'

'What's all this about then?'

'*Have* I?' Approaching the lift, they recognized the woman that emerged from it.

*

'Hello.'

'Morning, Mrs Winten. Nice morning.'

'Seen better,' Eddy said.

'Somebody called at your place a little while ago,' the woman said.

'Parson chap, I think.'

'Oh yes.'

'Asked me how long you'd be, as though I knew all about everything.'

'And you don't *know* all about everything,' Eddy snapped back. Ignoring this, the woman drew nearer to Lil. 'See 249's gone off again, Mrs Winten. That's three of them in the last six months.'

'Got it on the brain,' Eddy said, 'but there's a lot of it about these days.'

'I suppose there is, Mr Winten.'

'Let's get,' Eddy said. The lift whirred. They looked at each other and were silent. They got out, went quickly down the corridor.

'Wonder what *he* wanted?' Eddy fumbled with his keys, and Lil, holding onto remnants of Ann, said, 'Who?'

'Collar back to front chap. Remember him calling here the day after *that* day?'

'I know.'

'What he want with you, Lil, anyhow?'

'How'd I know that? He went on up to the flat above.'

'What's he want with us then? Christ! The way you keep getting plastered with something you don't want,' and he thrust the key into the lock. 'Might've been worse, of course,' suddenly mollifying.

'What does that mean?'

'The helmet coming back maybe, *that's* what. Had enough of it.'

'Let's get *in*,' she shouted, and pushed in front of him, went direct to the bedroom, removed coat and hat, and from there rushed off to the kitchen.

'Where are you, Lil?' after the door closed.

'Kitchen. Where else? Nearly dinner time.'

'Okay.' He followed her in, found her bent over the stove.

'Have to eat in spite of everything,' she said.

'Course,' and Eddy sat down. She talked out of the back of her head, stirred a pan violently.

'Did you really want to come out this morning?'

'Of *course.*'

'And you didn't mind Ann turning up like that, and won't mind her having a night here?'

'No.'

'No need to shout.'

'Sorry.'

'So you should be. Here's your dinner.'

'Ta,' and he sat down. 'Nerves peeping out everywhere. You ought to see the doctor, Lil.' She sat down, and they ate in silence. Eddy mused. 'She hates something all of a sudden, I know what it bloody is, too,' and he looked at her again, a changed woman in three days.

'Eat it up,' Lil said.

'I am eating,' he said.

'I'll be glad when it's all over,' Lil said.

'Telling me. And what the hell does that parson want? People as has come here since it happened.' He pushed away his plate. 'Nice.'

'Listen,' and she sat up.

'What?'

'*Listen.*'

'Somebody in her flat,' Eddy said. 'Now who could that be?'

'That probation lot probably. Checking up.'

'Checking *up*?'

'Mrs Biddulph told me they're selling Mrs Kavanagh's things, giving what they get to her. Understood.'

'*Very* nice,' Eddy said, then laughed, '*and* she'll blow it as soon as she gets out.'

'*If* she does. Third time this year.'

'Can't do anything with people like that, Lil. Really can't. Admire their patience.'

'I'm off,' Lil said.

'Right,' and they both got up, she went to the bedroom and he returned to the sitting room, sat down, carefully studied the *Radio Times*, finding out what they were going to offer them in the coming week.

'Ought to *kill* Finlay,' he exclaimed aloud, and flung the *Radio Times* across the room.

'Off now, dear.'

'Rightho.' The door banged. Eddy paced the room, suddenly loaded with resolutions. 'I'll not leave here, not for her or anybody else. Bloody mad.' He sat down just as the bell rang. 'Now who the hell's that?'

'Oh!' he said, the door wide. 'Yes. What is it?'

'Has Mrs Laurent arrived yet?'

'Mrs *Laurent*?'

'Said she'd be here.'

'*Where?* Oh, I see. Then you'd better go and have a look see, hadn't you.'

The caller said thank you, and Eddy said nothing.

'Getting his nose in, soul saving,' he thought, and heard the next flat door open and close. 'Must be there then. The goings on in this building. No end to it at all.' When the bell rang a second time, Eddy swore, but it was only Lil returned with the shopping.

'There you are,' and he relieved her of the load.

'Somebody next door,' Lil said.

'I know,' and he took the shopping into the kitchen.

'Where are you?' he called, and she wasn't there, and the front door wide. When he looked out his wife was stood at the partly opened inside window of the Kavanagh flat.

'Damn,' said Eddy, and slammed the door.

*

So the words came up into damp air, floated towards the window, hit Lil.

'Her world was made of cardboard,' he said, and fingers lifted and dropped some letters in a box. His name was Tench. Then heavily, '*yes*', and he did not look up.

Lil watched, and was still, listening, and she knew they had not seen her.

'*Well!*' she said. Eddy's head peeped out of the door. 'Lil?' She came, and he said sharply, 'For God's sake, woman. Standing at a bloody window listening to that lot,' so the door slammed again. And next door the man seated at the table laid his hand over the cardboard box.

'Extraordinary,' he said.

The groper after facts and the healer of wounds; the optimist with the soft centre was stood with her back to him, holding in the air a black coat, by tipped fingers, and once nostril near so that she suddenly exclaimed, 'Oh!' and let the garment fall to the floor, soundless.

'They should bury her in this,' Mrs Laurent said, and again he did not look up, and remained silent.

'I first read about it in the paper,' Tench said, 'realized who she was, remembered her,' and he stared about the room, then cast his eye at the little pile of clothing on the floor, and the piled furniture.

'The machinery of misery,' he thought. Mrs Laurent at last sat, opened her bag, took out a coffee flask, so she shared it, and sat opposite him at the table.

'Did you know Mrs Kavanagh very well?' she asked.

'Worked for me at one time,' he said, 'but not for very long. Must have been around sixty then. I had to get rid of her.'

'People have been getting rid of Mrs Kavanagh for quite some time,' Mrs Laurent said, then sipped.

'Lived for nothing else but the drink,' Tench said.

'I know.'

'A mystery to me. I never found out who she really was, or where she came from. She spoke loudest when her mouth was wet from the bottle.' He sighed, added, 'And I still don't know anything about her.'

'She'd had this friend for the last ten years, and it was something in her life.'

'And they say *she's* in now,' Tench said. So she looked fixedly at the saviour of souls, the man with the net.

'Quite harmless, my wife said, at the time,' he said.

'Both were, and that was the difficulty.'

'I admire the work you try to do, Mrs Laurent.'

'Thank you,' and rather stiffly. 'Not everybody does.'

'Of course. An extraordinary climate in which we live these days.' The observation intrigued her, but she did not pursue it.

'What did you say the lady's name was?'

'Biddulph,' Mrs Laurent said. 'More coffee?'

'No thank you,' and he picked up some letters out of the box, then let them fall again. 'All written when she was drunk.'

'She never wrote anything when she was sober, except the x she drew on a piece of paper once a week.'

'A very secret life,' he said.

'A lonely one.'

'Yes.' Mrs Laurent's arm rose, a hand swept across the room.

'If this lot fetches more than ten pounds, I'll be surprised.'

'Pathetic,' he said. 'Do you want these letters back?'

'We never want anything back,' she said.

'I'd have liked to see this Mrs Biddulph,' he said.

'She wouldn't like to see you,' Mrs Laurent said. 'I'm sure of that.' She put down the coffee cup, got up, and continued her examination of the contents of Mrs Kavanagh's home.

'These are the kind of legacies we sometimes get,' she said, and said it in her most authoritative manner, and he was quick to note it. 'You live hereabouts?'

'Behind St Jude's. Nobody comes these days, though we try to keep a few words alive.'

'I understand. I believe they both of them worked in some big house near Maida Vale.'

'Yes, but she came to us after that.'

'She left a curious note,' she said.

'I heard about it. Poor woman.' He made to rise, suddenly sat down again. 'And you don't want these,' and he lifted up the box.

'Not at all. Found in the cupboard there. Hidden away by her companion.'

'None are dated.' So Mrs Laurent was forced to laugh into the damp room and say, 'She wouldn't know one date from another. She was rarely sober.'

He fingered a letter. 'My wife is very interested in this sort of thing.'

'Indeed.'

'I shan't hold you up any longer,' Tench said. 'Is there anything I can do to help?'

'Nothing at all,' and the very tone of her voice dismissive.

'Very well. I'd still like to talk to this Mrs Biddulph.'

'It won't happen, Reverend,' Mrs Laurent said, and he read the finality in it.

'Cold this morning,' he said.

'It is cold.'

'Well, I'll be off.'

'Goodbye.' But he paused at the door, suddenly walked to the window, looked out.

'High,' he said.

'Very,' and she waited for him to go.

'And this is everything,' he said.

'Kitchen and another room,' she said, and watched him go to the door, open it, disappear, return in an instant.

'Empty,' he said.

'This room was her home,' Mrs Laurent said, and looked at her watch. 'My scrapman's late.'

'Selling up?'

'That's right. Buy a couple of bottles for her friend,' Mrs Laurent said, smiled at him, waited for one that would come, but he did not smile, and he did not think her observation very funny. She stood there, studying him. A big man, violent red hair, probably in his forties, and thought 'St Jude's', where on earth was that?

'Fancy your reading about it in the paper,' she said.

'It *is* news.'

'But almost everything's happening these days, Reverend,' she said. 'Do you visit the flats very often?'

He threw it off, casual: 'I come when I'm wanted.'

'A better time to come would be when you're *not*,' she replied, added quickly, 'Aren't you taking her life with you?'

'Of course,' he said, getting a grip on the box. 'And you're sure they're not wanted?'

She slowly shook her head, seemed on the point of smiling. 'Nobody wants them,' and then she forgot that he was there, moved about the room, counting things, checking. 'Miserable,' she said.

'What's that?'

'Nothing,' she said, leaden.

'Well, goodbye,' Tench said, 'and thank you,' and she saw him out and closed the door. 'A life under his arm. Probably amuse him.' The bell rang.

'Yes?' He was short, squat, stood four square at the door. 'Knawle,' he said.

'Mr Knawle.'

'That's it lady, scrap.'

She moved aside, 'You'd better come in.'

'Ta. This it?'

'That's it.'

He stood back, surveyed what he saw, then moved, bent down, stood up, moved on, paused, felt things, picked things up and put them down again, turned quickly. 'You *are* Mrs Laurent?'

'Should I be someone else? How much?'

'Fiver the lot,' Knawle said.

'*Five pounds?*'

'That's it, lady.'

'*Really.*'

'Rubbish. Not worth carrying away,' he said.

'It's a home,' she said.

'Not as I'd look at it, lady. Take it or leave it.'

'Dis*gus*ting. Five fifty,' she said.

He shook his head, dropped the words. 'Five pounds, and my engine's running, lady, we all have to make a living.'

'Five fifty.'

'Not worth it,' and he shrugged shoulders, made for the door.

'*Very* well.'

'You've the authority? All kinds of folk going about these days.' She pulled out a card from her bag, showed it him.

'D'you want it, or *don't* you?' she said. His hand went to his pockets, and she watched the money come out. Dirty, well-used, he slipped one clear of the mess, handed it to her.

'Thanks, lady,' after which he rushed to the door, called, 'Dave!' Dave, waiting on the threshold, came, and Knawle said, 'That's it.'

'Taking it *now*?' she asked.

'Course.'

She sat down on an empty wooden box. 'Take it.' She watched Knawle and Son deal very efficiently with Kavanagh fragments.

'What an end.'

And Knawle and Son rushed in and out as though every second were loaded. She was glad to get up and close the door behind them. The emptiness increased the silence. It made her think of a high wind, quickly in and out. She went into stripped kitchen, room, closed doors after her, sat on the box. *Everything*. Finished. She picked up her bag and left the flat.

The lift being out of order *again*, she passed Knawle and Son on the stairs, and they did not notice her as she went by. The very sight of her car raised spirits, and she was glad to get into it. She sat back in the seat, fingering the wheel, her foot handy, but she did not move. Staring out through the windscreen, she thought of Holloway, and another charge, and Biddulph waiting, for anything. And the first meeting, after she had been lifted.

'A sorry business, Mrs Biddulph,' and Mrs Biddulph looked right through her, and said nothing.

'How long did you say you'd known her?'

'Told you.'

'Tell me again.'

'Met her in the gutter ten years ago. D'you have to be told everything *twice* all in a breath?'

'What exactly did she do?'

'She was in kitchens half over London before I copped up with her.'

'Which kitchens?'

'Anybody's, everybody's. Okay then?'

'But didn't you work together Maida Vale way?'

'First I've heard of it. Who told you that. Bloody fib, could tell a few if she wanted, poor thing.'

'What part of Ireland did she come from?'

'Never said. Wouldn't. She was like that, too.'

'D'you ever hear from your people, Mrs Biddulph?'

'*No*. Thank Christ.'

'No need to shout.'

'You asked me.'

'Seems to have been born on a piece of paper,' she paused, 'like that son of hers.'

'Nothing to do with you. That's *private*.'

'So she *hadn't* a son.'

'No. She hadn't. What's it all about? What does it matter *now*?'

'Keep your voice down, and try to remember what has happened.'

'I'm remembering, must think me bloody stupid.'

'Control yourself.'

'Sorry.'

'That's better.'

'Never told me where she worked, how long she'd been down here, never did anything from the day she picked up the pension. Neither did I. Okay? Free country, isn't it?'

'How did you *live*?'

'Just lived.'

'Ten years is a long time.'

'Been in and out long before I knew her. Sometimes she'd go out in the morning, be away the whole day, worried me, then she told me she'd been down to Tilbury, used to like to sit watching the ships. Then she'd come back, and always something in her pocket, and we'd *have* that soon's we were set down and cosy. Slept in her big coat if it was cold. Once told me she had a man, didn't last long though, said he left her standing on a quay . . .'

'Where?'

'How do I know.'

'But for the fact of the pension nobody would ever have heard of her,' Mrs Laurent said.

'Some people don't want to be heard of, why should they if they don't bloody want to?'

'She really believed in this son of hers.'

'*Real*. Lived for him, talked about nothing else from the day he come up out of the tealeaves. D'you know what, Mrs, tell you. I once thought he was in the kitchen with us, so real that time, like he was leaning over your shoulder. Ah! Made her happy, at the time, I mean. What's wrong with that?' A pause, and a sudden, unexpected confidence. 'We've sat in every park in London. Just think of that.'

'You wrote the letters for her,' Mrs Laurent said, calm, casual.

'Once wrote a long one herself. Wasn't much at the writing though. I remember you wrote one for her yourself, when I was "in" that time. She told me. Told me everything.'

'I did.'

'Well then?'

'I found the letters.'

'*Found* them?'

'Back of the cupboard.'

'Oh God! No . . .' Mrs Biddulph said.

'Something the matter?'

'I'll have to think about it, that's all. Should be torn up. Bloody silly, quite mad some of them.'

'We'll burn them.'

'Glad.'

'Why are you glad?'

'My business.'

The Laurent hand, suddenly lying across her own, surprised her.

'I am really sorry about this, Mrs Biddulph, I mean your

being here,' and added with some emphasis, 'you know who I am.'

'So'm I,' Mrs Biddulph replied, got up, pushed away the hand. 'You told her I'd been lifted, didn't you?'

'I never told anybody anything, my dear,' Mrs Laurent said.

'Don't want any cod stuff from you.'

'You're not getting any. Have you made any plans?'

'Plans?'

'They may let you go tomorrow.'

'Fancy.'

'Tell me, Mrs Biddulph, who *was* the last person to whom you said thank you?' Mrs Biddulph turned her back on the woman, stared at the wall. 'Well?' Words came out of the back of her head.

'Last person I said thank you to was a chap at Soonan's, because he was so blind at the time. Anything else?' and she followed this up with a pronounced titter.

'I've been very patient with you.'

'I've been patient with everybody all my bloody life. Think of *that*!' and she swung round, glared at Mrs Laurent. 'And so was she, too, *and* you know who I mean.'

'That's enough.'

'Course. You lot know everything, and more than that. Why don't you run away and leave people alone?' She hated the proffered smile, seemed not to hear the Laurent reply.

'Sometimes I wish I could. Goodbye.' She thought of the deadly efficiency of Knawle and Son, of a tall man with red hair, remembered a conversation, his 'one tries to keep a few words alive', and immediately she saw the empty church, Tench hoping. Goodness didn't seem to be enough. She slowly shook her head, put her foot down, screamed round the corner.

VI

TENCH, box under his arm, made his way to the small, quiet house at the rear of St Jude's. His head inside the door, and the usual call.

'Children gone off, dear?' And the expected answer. 'Gone.'

'It *was* her,' Tench said, entering the hall.

'Was it?'

'Yes.' He put the box down on the chair, and entered the room. His wife was motionless on the couch, silent behind *The Times*, and this was lowered the moment she knew he had sat down.

'Coffee?'

'Please,' he said, and the pipe out, and lighting it, and lying back, relaxed. 'Been at Totall for nearly three years. Didn't even know. Knew I was right.'

'Oh!' she said, distantly, hovered over him, 'glad you went anyway.'

'I *do* happen to have a few members of congregation at Totall Point,' and she was quick to note a pained look.

'I'll get coffee.'

'Do.' She called from the hall. 'What is this?'

'Oh! Some odd papers they found at the back of her cupboard. Her few things were being sold up when I got there. Depressing. One was sitting in the world's room.' He heard her go into the kitchen, humming a sudden tune, quite lost on him, of no importance. She came back, served.

'Fancy your not knowing she was there in three years, Luke,' she said. Her name was Vera.

'Buildings like that simply *hide* people. Another foot and the poor woman would have been living on the roof.'

'Some people liked them at first,' Vera said, 'but now some of them are changing their minds about cosmic living.'

'More coffee, dear?' He shook his head. She got up and went into the hall, brought back the small cardboard box. 'May I?'

'Why not,' and he watched her dip fingers into the box, lift out a few letters written on cheap notepaper, and nearly all, written in ink.

'Why d'you want them?' she asked.

'A life,' he thought, and then, 'Merely curiosity,' he replied. 'They were due for the rubbish chute. I looked through some of them. She let me have them in the end. Nice woman.'

'What about her connections?'

'None.'

'Friends?'

'Seems to have only had the one, and I was told that she herself is back in again.'

'None of them are dated,' she said.

'I noticed that.'

'Awful writing.'

'It's pretty awful,' he said, got up, picked up the box. 'I'm going to my study,' he said, and immediately left the room. Vera cleared up after him. She heard his study door close, and immediately called out:

'I'll be out till noon, dear.'

'Very well,' he called back, sat down, emptied the cardboard box, and before flinging it to the wastepaper basket read the goods advertised. 'Morlans hygienic teats.' He picked up a letter, opened it, read, 'My dear Sean . . .'

stopped, put it down, sat back, and thought about the writer.

Someone living precariously, sustained by pieces of paper. Unknown, uncertain, an accident; he thought of stray pigeons descending noiselessly into Trafalgar Square. He picked up the letter, began again.

My dear Sean,

I was so sorry that I didn't write you for so long, but I was in again, and I worried about that, but my friend Lena Biddulph came to see me and she said she'd drop you a line about how I was going on, which was much as usual, but I was miserable in there. I mean not being able to do the things I like to do. Funny the way it happened though. I'd gone off to Tilbury to look at the ships there, of course I used to go off to other docks as well, but devil a ship with a blue funnel could I see. Once, I dreamed I saw you up the funnel, painting it, the same blue it was as some curtains I once had, a beautiful blue they were. I was so worried case you came down, I mean fell down, which you didn't in the end, thank God. I hope this letter finds you well, and as happy as one is allowed to be these days. Well, I was just sitting on this bench, looking out over the river, and you wouldn't believe this, my dear son, but it was the very same policeman as last time, and he came up to me and sat down. He looked at me for a long time, and then he said, 'Hadn't you better get off home now, madam, it's not very warm today. Get along now,' he said, but I didn't budge an inch, wasn't doing any harm to anybody, but he just went on and on, and once I thought he'd push me off the bench. 'Come along now,' he said, and the next moment he had me on my feet and was leading me off, stupid man, I was happy where I was, always am, till these people come along. 'You're drunk, madam,' he said, and if you don't get off home I'll have to do something about it, which he did of course, because I wasn't going for anybody. I was just sitting there quiet, looking at ships. So it was how it was, and they had me in again. I keep thinking about you, my dear son, and the way I go on wishing you were here, ah, but you'd never *really* know how much. My friend Lena told me the other day that if I go on writing letters like this they'll come and take me away, and put me in one of those mad-houses, awful, I thought she was cruel, saying it, because usually she isn't like that. Yesterday I stood looking out of the window where I am, and I *wished* you'd come round the corner, quick, a surprise, I'd have gone on my tiptoes to shout your name out of the window. Love that I would, since people round here think I haven't a son at all, that's what they're like these days, can't even dream about nice things happening these times. Do write to me, I wish to *God* you would. There's such a nice man at the post office round the corner, Mr Denton I think he is, always gives me a smile when I call to see if a letter's turned up, and the way he says it, 'sorry, dear, nothing for you today.' I think he's good, and that's why I believe him. Sometimes I'm sad when I go out, so my friend and I, we go off to a place called The Marquis, cheers you up there. Just love doing that, forget who you are for a whole evening, lovely . . .

'Pathetic,' he said, picked up his pipe, lit it, dropped the letter. Vera came back, banged a door, flew to a kitchen, was suddenly busy. And again she hummed a tune, and again Tench did not hear it. And he knew it didn't matter, and he ran his fingers amongst other letters, picked up another, by chance a short one, read.

My dear Son,

Not much today. Sorry, but as I told you once I'll tell you everything that happens, I'm telling you. Bloody lucky to do it, you'd never know. Last night it was, half eleven I think, on my own, coming away from The Lantern, that's near a Darby and Joan place, the noise, they were doing their usual knees up stuff, bloody childish *I* thought, so I came on past there and had just got to the bottom of Winkley St, turning the corner, when somebody had me against a wall in a tick, and a fist like a plate back of my neck and words in my ear that horrified me. 'Drop it, old tot,' he said, I wondered what till I felt my bag in my hand, the clutch I had on it, he pressed hard on my hand, 'drop the bloody thing,' he said, and gave my head a little knock against the wall but I still held onto it, *was* mine. It was like spit in my ear in a flash, and he said, 'be sensible old woman, knock you if you shout,' so I was sensible, opened my hand, dropped the bag, he grabbed it, ran off, I stood, still, drained I was then, *drained*. Went on home, said nothing at all to Lena, wouldn't, enough's enough, but I hardly slept that night, thought I'd die once, just the shock of it. Ah well. No more bad news. God bless you, my dear son, your loving mother. P.T.O.

He turned a page.

Remembered my bag, everything in it, was angry just thinking about it, key, two penny stamps, two blessed snowdrops, had them years, Father Houlihan five years ago, gone now, poor man, piece of paper and my instructions what to do with me when I'm gone, a sixpence the swine will never find, had to go to the bloody council lot about a new key. Got it.

The name came, sing-song across the hall. 'Lu-uke.'

'There you are then,' he said, rose quickly from another world, met her in the kitchen. 'Glad you're back. Just read an extraordinary letter, quite extraordinary. What a big dream she had, nicest thing about it.'

'What on earth are you talking about, dear?' Vera said, looked up from the table at which she was now very busy.

'Doesn't matter,' he said, and then, quite involuntarily, 'she was good with the children, whilst it lasted.'

'I was always afraid for the children,' Vera said, cutting, final.

'A harmless creature . . .'

'But the *drink* . . .'

'Yes, dear. I know. Shall we quietly forget about it, shall we?' and a big smile, and sitting opposite her, and being helpful. And he helped, and the smile was welcome.

'When is it, dear?' tentatively, and he said quietly, 'Tomorrow. For some reason she always remembered Willesden. I often think of that rectory these days. Nicer than this one.'

'Yes,' absent-mindedly, 'I suppose it was, dear.'

'Leave you to it,' Tench said, and went back to the study. He stood over the desk, fingered the letters, picked up another, began reading, dropped it, put them all together, then safely away in the drawer. In an instant closing and opening of the eyes she was there, *in* the room, the hall at Willesden.

'I remember, a hot morning, August, there she was, shading her eyes, wilting where she stood.'

'Wicked, Mrs Kavanagh, wicked.'

'Sorry, Mr Tench.'

'It's still *wicked*.' Saw the mouth still wet, from communion wine.

'I knew the *stuff*, sir, long before I knew the holy water.

I'm sorry, sir. Forgive me.' Thought of the shame in her, bent low, heard her beginning to cry. The waved hand, the pat on the shoulder.

'Forget it, Mrs Kavanagh,' I said, 'just forget it.' And the bleat, 'How can I, sir?'

'Try.'

'Yes, sir.' Watched her go, bent, diminished, listless arms, head so down, only the neck visible, watched her climb stairs, hide in her room.

'The children loved her, we didn't.' He got up, crossed to the window, looked out on roof and more roof. Vera called, breaking the silence. 'In your study, dear?'

'Yes.' He came out. 'Anything the matter, dear?'

'Nothing,' a long pause, and then, 'd'you have to go, Luke?'

'Yes,' he said, prompt, being near to a death.

'Doesn't matter, really,' she said, and he said nothing, was glad.

'I must glance at the paper,' he said, dropped her hand, went in to the sitting room, sat down. Before the headlines screamed at him he looked up, and then a thin smile. 'I was just thinking of the time she stole the communion wine.'

'Awful.'

'Sad,' he said, 'just sad.' She, too, sat, dawdled her fingers in a work basket, wondered if she would knit, saw him lost behind *The Times*.

'Luke?'

'What, dear?' wearily.

'Your collars, you won't forget,' she said.

'Won't forget,' saw Vera, *not* forgetting, practical Vera, and a philosophy summed up inside the words. 'Play safe any time.' Words climbed over the paper, this moved slightly, as though he would drop it in an instant.

'I can remember once when she very badly wanted to

talk to you, dear, and somehow you just didn't seem to be around . . .'

'Probably busy,' she said, picked up some unfinished knitting.

'You always are, dear. Still, I was sorry about it at the time.'

'That's *long* ago, dear. Why do you keep harping on it?' He said nothing, turning a page. He heard the sudden click of needles and with some relief. He turned more pages, without reading, words inside clashing with those without.

'Just blowing about the world like a piece of paper,' he thought, dropped *The Times* in a heap, got up, reassembled it, folded and put it down, turned towards the door.

'I thought you'd finished, dear,' Vera said, not looking up.

'I'm never finished,' he said, and went straight back to his study. The drawer wanted to be open, the letters wanted to come out, he sat down, put them on his desk, casually opened one, put on his spectacles. The year, the month and the day, dead. The moment mattering. He read.

My dear son,

I can't quite remember if I sent off my letter to you last Wednesday, but I hope I did, as I'm sure you'd be disappointed if you didn't hear from me. Again the answer for me was 'no', such a big *no*, so again I'm patient, just waiting. Went off to Benediction last night but my knees went half way through so I come home again. She's still 'in', my friend I mean, poor woman, she's just like me, can't help it anytime. Always glad the cupboard's there, the stuff in it. Saves you. I'd expected gin, she brought beef. Did I tell you about that place opening round here, Soonan's it is, shop's as big as a town, you get lost in it. Poor Lena she just *can't* keep away from the bloody place. Oughtn't to tempt people like they do. Wouldn't ever touch a line like that, pay for what I like, always have, keeps you going all the time, and sometimes it's worse when you're *forced* to keep going, you know what I mean. Tell me d'you still have that big lock of hair that used to stick hard to your forehead? Often wondered. I'll always know that your eyes are brown, always remember that lot.

He paused when the pause came, a line of gibberish, and thought, and smiled with it, 'perhaps it came after the last shot from the bottle.' He continued.

I was thinking the other night of all the places I've been to in London, the kitchens I ran around in, made me *feel* tired just thinking about it, so I stopped at once. Just sitting down was nicer there. Did you get my friend's letter, Lena, I mean, she said she'd written you a letter, just before she went in? She *is* kind, even though I sometimes think she's a doubtful lot, left her family behind up in some place called Leeds, reckon her family threw her out, you can't believe everything, though that sort of thing happens a lot these days. Fancy some spit of a daughter saying to her, 'get!' Just like that. Ah . . .! Did Lena tell you about how we've sat in every park in London, and how once she got copped by a park-keeper? God, it was only two flowers and a few leaves. Never in my life have I seen such a pig of a man. Enough of that. Remember once I asked you to tell me everything about the *Devonian*, but I know you're busy, can't always, all the same I'd love it. All about the ship, the people on it, where she goes. Mr Denton said there are some ships that are away for years, and never in any one port more than a day, the ship people being hungry for the cargoes they want so badly. I hope the captain is a nice man. Not everybody is these days and you have to be *so* careful. The funnel is blue, isn't it, and there's just one single stripe round that. Those letters M.V. are a complete mystery to me, wonder what they mean, tell me next time you write. Christ! Sometimes I just feel like shouting right across the seas, 'write soon'. It's the way things get you, might be the day, or a dead evening. It's always best when Lena's out again. I never *never* go near The Marquis place when she's in, but slip into The Lantern, quiet there, and you can sit in a corner there and stay shut up as long as you want. Sorry about the writing, my *dear* son, gets like that when I'm without the stuff too long. Way it goes. Funny the dream I had last night, strange in a way, because there was a man in it, great big feller he was, was him that left me standing once on a cold quay, the *bastard*, can't say less, really and I'm glad as *glad* he was never your father, dear. Ah! Imagine me waking up quick out of another dream, and God, there you are, real, close, at last, and the strong hand, and *feeling* it, so warm, makes me warm just thinking about it sometimes.

Vera, who was dutiful, never forgot anything, called, 'Nearly time, dear,' and Tench didn't hear, close to a near spent voyage, in among the worn, now warm, filthy pieces of paper, secure in their own ink.

'Are *you* coming, dear?'

'In a minute,' not thinking of the minute and what it contained, or where Vera was, what she was doing at this very moment, so he turned a page, the longest letter of them all, continued to read, bent close to the paper, as though spectacles were insufficient for it, requiring sight beyond that of eyes.

'*Luke!*'

'I said I'm *coming*, dear,' irritable, frustrated, a fugitive thought, 'perhaps this letter will be without end.' Dropped it, got up, ran out, straight into the dining room, and she was in it, a duty done.

'Thought you'd never come, dear,' Vera said. 'Still reading?' And he said, parrot-like, 'yes,' imaginary hands flailing cloud, trying to surface, surfacing, back to known air, hearing the clock tick. They ate. Occasional glances at Tench, he unaware, and the too sudden question. He paused, looked up. 'Did you say something, dear?'

'No. But I've been wondering, Luke, about this year's holiday.' A foreign word, after the long voyage. 'What about it?' he asked.

'I don't want Bournemouth again,' Vera said.

'Oh! I see. Broadstairs?' He paused, then jerked out, 'Or how about Scotland for a change?'

'Everybody seems to be going to Scotland this year,' replied Vera.

'All right then. I'll think about it, dear,' he said. The words were wrong, for climate and moment, but he uttered them, as though a puzzle had been solved, Vera no longer there.

'So secret when she was sober,' he said. She caught the clue like lightning. 'Oyster, dear,' Vera said.

'The letters fascinate me,' he said, continued his lunch, head down, as though ignoring her.

'So many things appear to fascinate you, dear,' Vera said, the words with razor edge.

'My job.' So she, too, in a moment signalled she was clam, ate in silence, did not again look up, both aware of a clock's tick, and she thinking of Joan, Sophia, he thinking of secretless secrets, in another world.

'You'll meet the children as usual?' she asked, the perennial lunch-hour ultimatum.

'Yes.'

'Good.'

'You know the Evelyns are coming Wednesday, dear?'

'Yes.' She refrained from being automatic, repeating herself, gracefully rose. 'I'll get the coffee.' And he formal. 'Thank you.'

'Vera must yet learn what she is required to do, in extreme moments.' He pushed away his plate, absent-mindedly put pipe to lips, remembered, stuffed it into his pocket, just as his wife returned. Dawdling time again, like yesterday, tomorrow also, without a doubt, worn words stretching into dead afternoon, shattered at five by strident voices, high pitched, and the laughter, the house alive.

'Sugar?' she asked, like another duty to do.

'You know I don't take sugar, dear,' and took the coffee, and did not say thank you. Both sipped, into the silence, both knew the clock would soon strike.

'Bring back the cleaning, dear.'

'Of course.'

'I'll clear up now,' she said, and he said, 'rightho,' got up, went to the couch, sat, fingered knitting.

'What is this?'

'The jumper, dear.' Sensed his absent-mindedness, would not disturb it.

'You won't forget Wednesday, dear, the Evelyns?'

'Said I wouldn't.'

'You've been rather nervy lately, Luke, and even the children have noticed it.'

'Just upset about something, dear,' he said, and she did not ask him what it was. And the words that were casual, breaking a spell.

'World's full of people like Mrs Kavanagh,' Vera said, and got up, was hurriedly preoccupied with clearing the table, and never cleared it without recalling other days, brighter times, and the girl that would clear it for her. Tench's pipe positively oozed smoke.

'What will you do with them?' she asked.

'With what?'

'Those letters, dear.'

'Burn them,' he said, immediately got up. 'And I'll be busy until half three,' and left her gathering the table's contents.

'They must be very interesting, dear,' she called, as he went through to his study. He turned, paused a moment, looked at her, said nothing, went in, and the door soundlessly closed.

'I can't share his passion for everything,' she thought, absolved herself, obliterated a particular situation, carried everything to the kitchen, and for the first time in her life did not wash up, but went back to the sitting room, picked up her knitting, knitted furiously. The flashing needles morsed messages:

'I'd never have married anybody else. He is a good man, a responsible man, we *are* happy, the children are dears.' Yes, they were lucky. 'Time Luke had a change. He's quite right about Willesden. A beautiful place. I know he misses it, poor dear.' She accepted the silence that fell upon the room, enjoyed it. And a silence from the study, he being lost again, and the light beginning to go. He switched on the lamp, bent lower over the desk, picked up another letter.

'Not a single date anywhere.' And read:

Dear Sean,

First, don't worry about me if you haven't heard lately because I'm 'in' again, but not for long, the usual this time so as I'll know the exact day I'll be out again I've sent a message by a lady going *out* to that nice Mr Denton. If a letter's come and he has it, I know he'll send it along in. Excuse the shortest note I ever wrote, dear, somebody just coming along, and when somebody is coming along in *this* place, you know what it's all about. Keep well, son, I think of you every night, I pray for you. Even if I never see you, even if I never *will*, there's something that lights me up, just knowing you're there. I close my eyes, I stretch out my hand.

Your fond mother, Brigid Kavanagh.

As if praying, Tench said, 'What a beautiful letter.'

He thought of a friendship cut in two, tried to remember the name of the woman given him by Mrs Laurent, wondered about her, what she would do. 'I'd have liked to talk to her. A strange pair indeed.' He piled the letters, he counted them, 'Twenty-seven, twenty-eight, twen . . .'

'Time, dear,' Vera called, a tocsin ring through the house, the death of the afternoon.

VII

LIL was there, *again*, and the eye drowned in what it saw.

'Hello!'

'Hello!'

'Any news, dear?'

'None.'

'But there will be soon?'

'When the sods say there will,' Mrs Biddulph said. 'How are you, dear?'

'I'm all right, Mrs Bidd . . . I mean Lena, how are you?'

'How'd I look?'

The Biddulphian abruptness that broke out from time to time, unnerved Lil, made her uncertain of her thoughts, bewildered her whole nature, left her groping for the words that would do, survive the moments.

'That lot was here yesterday, Lil, it is Lil?' And the first smile.

'That's right, Lena.'

'Asked me if I was going off to Willesden. Think of that. Things they think of, things they *say*. In another world now, dear, don't we know.'

'I do hope everything comes all right, Lena,' Lil said.

'Can come to a thing too soon.'

'You can come to a thing too late, dear,' Lil said. 'Surely you should make plans for coming out. You haven't a settled place at the moment.'

'She said to me the other day they're selling up Brigid's

things, casual she was, the bitch, like she was just talking about the bloody weather. Riled me it did, *riled*.'

'I'm sorry.'

'Selling her stuff, think of that. Bit of charity stuck out then, like a bad tooth, really, said to me, "If you wished I could try and do something with the council about you having Mrs Kavanagh's place," Said nothing to that. Offered me what cash she picks up for what's left of somebody, and I mean *left*, everything so *close* to her, always was, told her she could put the bloody lucre where Paddy put the nuts.'

Lil sat back, closed eyes for a moment, the words repeating in her head.

'Lil?' And it travelled on a fairy breath. 'Lil?' and leaning in to the visitor, and offering her rarest of possessions, a smile. 'Remember you asked me something yesterday, something particular it was . . . Blast! Gone out of my head, d'you remember what?'

Lil didn't. 'D'you never hear from your people these days?'

'Never mattered, not after the look I got, my daughter I mean, name was Lily, like yours, if *that* look I got one February afternoon had been a bloody knife I'd have been dead in a tick. I shan't forget. Still trying to think of what it was you asked me about yesterday, still trying . . .' and one clenched fist hammered the table edge.

'*I* know,' Lil said.

'What was it, dear?'

'It was about when Mrs Kavanagh was ill one evening and you had to run out to The Marquis place.'

'That's it,' and a near jubilance in the Biddulph tone of voice.

'Tell you,' she said.

'Tell.'

'She was at Totall at the time, not long after they knocked

us at the little place we had in Gag Lane, never was a need for *that*, doesn't matter now anyhow I came up that evening, dark it was at the time, February I think but I'm not certain, was in a lodging place at the time . . .'

'Rowton?'

'That's *men*, no, just a place you could go to, women only of course and I'd just got back from a visit to George God, usual had-to stuff, worry themselves down to tuppence over your aches and bloody pains these days, welfare stuff, 'spect you know that anyhow with everybody mugging in on it. Funny though, never visited that feller without his having a mood on, I put it down to continuous indigestion, bile, something like that, never had a good mood on him, and I used to be sorry for a nice young chap as helped him there, Binks his name was, and one time I was there George was really angry about something and roared for this young chap who came rushing in waving a form, and said somebody named Miss Coolduck hadn't filled up the full form, funny name that, and George shouted in his ear when he looked at the form and shouted again at him how she hadn't filled in the H seven something, E L something else, roared him out of the room again, looked at me, said, "Now, about *you*". I was sorry for Binks, you could tell the young man was still new there, face still shining,' she paused suddenly, said, 'You all right, dear?' and Lil said, yes, she was. 'Well anyhow I came over to the Totall place, usual thing, if no lifts, crawl, if working float up. I was dead surprised when she opened the door, near fell on me with a sigh of relief. "Thought you'd never come," she said. "What's wrong?" I said, though I knew at once what it was . . .'

'What was it?'

'Ill, dear, real ill, and I mean *ill*.'

'What did you do, Lena?'

'Sat her down where she sort of drooped in the chair, pale she was, and sat there staring at nothing at all, tell she was nervy, way she shook when I touched her, knelt then, I said, "You're not ill, are you, Brigid?" and she said nothing. Rushed around, nothing in a pot, nothing in the cupboard which was much worse, knelt again. "How much you got, dear?" I asked her, and she said, "Purse there," but there was damn all in it, it was the purse that give me the answer so I said, "Won't be long, dear, stay put, don't you move, won't be a tick," rushed out, ran all the way to The Marquis, crowded it was that time of the evening, just rushed on down where Mr Finch was, end of the counter, caught his arm, said "Mr Finch". He looked at me, said "Anything wrong?" and I said "Yes, it's her, Mr Finch, *her*". Course he knew what I meant, and he said, "What's the matter, Mrs Biddulph?" so I told him the lot, worried I was, the way she looked at you when you asked her something, like you wasn't there. I pulled on Finch then so we got behind the red curtain end of the counter, I said, "You know what, Mr Finch," after which only one word left in my mouth, and I put my teeth on it, looked at him again, and then he knew what I meant. At once his expression changed and he said, "But what about last week, Mrs Biddulph?" and I let the word fly out of my mouth then. "*Please*," I said, pulled on his arm. He was cool as an iceberg the next minute, talked so casual, said, "Have you called the doctor?" "No," I said, "I didn't," and again I said, "*Please*. Just till Wednesday, Mr Finch." He looked at me, I looked at him, tell he was feeling for what he had to say and I was damned glad that evening that Mrs Finch wasn't too well herself, in bed upstairs, *she'd* been there would never have got it, never. "Mr Finch," I said, and he bent down over me and simply said, "*What*, Mrs Biddulph?" and all I said then was "*Give!*" '

'Did he?'

'A kind man, course Brigid and me were regulars there anytime, ah, I was glad he lived up to it, said, "Here, dear, and hurry off home, and don't forget next Wednesday, tell her I was asking after her," and I said, "Yes, thanks," and was gone in a tick and running like a bloody lunatic all the way back to Totall Point, took me half an hour to get up to her den, if it isn't the lifts there, it's the bloody lights, how it is, no questions asked, none answered, nobody says *nothing*, takes it, how it is, always will be *now*.' Lil had stiffened slightly in the chair, was silent, clasped hands heavy in her lap, islanded in the flood of words that had flowed across the table.

'She did get better then?'

'Hadn't moved an inch from the time I left her, and drooped there still only lower, like you'd think she'd bend in half any minute. I propped her up, I said, "It's all right. Seen the doctor, got the medicine." Never moved, never even looked at me, sort of wilted and stayed like that in the chair, stiff with something, and her mouth tight shut. I was *so* sorry for her then, poor dear. I knocked the top and had the stuff going down, and I took a strong nip myself, and I watched and waited, but still not a wink nor a move out of her, knew it was just sheer bloody lack of the stuff, you see some weeks were good and some were bad, all expected, the way things went with us, and never a real surprise, left you feeling worse than lost some days. She moved. God! Was I glad, moved in the chair, began sitting up, but oh, so slowly, thought she'd never do it, half-closed eyes she had, "Ah, that's better, Brigid," I said, and sent down another bright message for her. Knew the medicine had done the trick.

' "Glad you're here, Lena," was all she said, and no need for me to say a word, *not* a single word. Took another chair, sat by her, held her hand, feel the warmth coming back, near cold when I ran out and left her. "You better lie down," I said, and she looked up for the first time, and her eyes wide, and at last, the smile. Did you good to see it. "I thought you were going to die on me, dear," I said, squeezed her hand, and she squeezed back, so it was like things were normal again, the evening back on its feet as you might say. "All right now, dear?" She smiled. "Sure?" And she smiled again. "I'll make tea," I said, always liked a good hot strong cup of tea with the stuff. Couldn't have done it with gin. One day when she's fully clear of the stuff, and the breath of it I'll tell her how kind Finch was. I made tea.'

Mrs Biddulph paused, took a long look at the visitor, half rose, leaned over her, and said very quietly, 'You wouldn't ever believe this, Lil,' hand seeking hand again, 'never. I always dreaded the moment, really, for it only had to be her drunk, and me some way off it, before the whole bloody thing started again, knew it was coming, *knew*. She sort of buried her head in the teacup, said, "Did I write to Sean last Wednesday, Lena?"

'Felt choked, couldn't say anything for a minute, then I snapped, "Yes, you did. What about it?" sort of snapped it at her, curious it was, but in that very second I was saying to myself, "Well my God!" And I meant it, yes, it must come to a bloody end, I'm sick of it, I'm sick of the cup and the leaves and the dream and the bloody light that comes with it. I *really*, honestly, felt choked by the bloody lot of it, and I shouted in her face, "I'm sick to bloody death of your son, sick of it all," and it *was* the way I felt *then*, just *couldn't* help saying it.' A long pause, and she dragged the remaining words.

'I could have cut my bloody throat the moment I said it. She cried, God, the way she cried. Held her tight, said nothing, knew what I was holding, knew it was real to her, knew she'd never forget, knew she'd hang on to the son, fingers and hands and arms and teeth, and *claws* if you like.'

Mrs Biddulph sat back in the chair, unclenched her hands, and they vanished under the table. Very abruptly she said, 'You haven't said anything, Lil, not anything.'

'What shall I say?' thought Lil. 'What shall I ask? What can I do?'

'Too late to be sorry for her, Lena, but not too soon for you. And I *am* sorry. It must have been terrible, it really must.' The sudden break in the Biddulph voice shocked her.

'Only wanted to be happy, only wanted to go on writing and writing and writing to one that was dead as a stone. Not much to ask for, really. Simple enough. Ah! . . . you'll never really know, dear.'

'I do understand, Lena,' Lil said. The reply was swift, nail sharp. '*Ta*.'

'What a life,' thought Lil, looked up the room, down the room, wondered what would come, again glanced at the clock, met the watching eye.

'You'll know tomorrow then?'

'Know today.'

'That's good. I hope they clear you, Mrs Biddulph. Pity in a way you didn't accept that offer, I mean about your having Mrs Kavanagh's place. Be next to us then. You wouldn't be lonely,' a quick vision of charity, the words free flowing, she *longed* to help.

'Nice of you,' Mrs Biddulph said.

'Not at all.'

'I said it's nice of you, and it is,' Mrs Biddulph said.

'How long ago was that?' Lil asked.

'Does it matter? Doesn't. Never forget it all the same, first time her and me ever had a row at all, like sisters we were, really, then she exploded, shouted in my face. "Damn you, Lena Biddulph," so I said it back at her, "Then damn you, too," I said, and I lifted my coat from the hook, beat it. Let it rage itself off her, beat it for the nearest bus stop, sat on a bench there, huddled I was, angry with her yet sorry at the same time, never should have happened, just sat on and on watching people come and go, only got up when it got real damp. Walked very slowly back to Totall, thinking all the way there. Could have kicked myself every step I took, got back, went on up, door half open, anybody could have darted in, nicked the lot, shut the door after me, wondered where she'd gone. Got myself a warmer-up, sat, waited for her, bound to come after they're all shut, she . . .'

'But if she hadn't any money,' Lil said, correcting.

'She'd get it with less than nothing, think of that, shows how bad it was, how she just *had* to have the stuff, ah, she'd get it all right. Came back at a quarter past eleven, never spoke a single word to me, just walked past, went to bed, covered herself up, put the light out. That's how it was. Next day I heard she'd gone straight into The Lantern, sat herself in a corner, manager told me about it, she wasn't his regular, she'd just drop in, sit there, saying nothing, the stuff in front of her. When he told me about it I really wanted to laugh, but I didn't.

'The place was pretty packed, he said, Dolan his name was, and they had the tele on, Fulham playing at home that evening, he said, and then she walked right in, went to a dark corner sat there, barman came, knew her by sight, thought she still looked ill, paid for a drink for her, left her. Never believe what happened after that. Expect it was just the way she looked, *then*. She shouted at the top of her voice, "I don't know who I am," course everybody laughed then, and Dolan said, leaning over her, "I think you're a silly old woman, why don't you go home." She laughed in his face then. Nobody else did. Not a soul there laughed with her. Dolan raised her to her feet, led her to the door, and told her that one of these days she'd be getting put into the bin. It was then she came on back. Went to her room door, she was snoring. The relief, just hearing her at it. But I was still mad with myself, more I thought about it, it was what I said, way I said it, "I'm sick of your bloody son". '

'I do understand, Lena,' Lil said, trying to, lost in a fog of words.

'Glad somebody does. I think you're decent, that's what, coming here like this, won't forget some time, promise you that, very good of you to do it, real nice. Complete stranger to you, dear.'

Lil rewarded this with an expansive smile, reached for the Biddulph hand, laid it in her own, stroked it with another.

'Glad I came. Glad I knew, dear.'

There was warmth in the titter. 'So'm I.'

'Promise me something, Lena.'

'What?'

'That if they let you go, you'll remember where I live. And Eddy'll understand. Always does.'

'Husband?'

'That's right.'

'Family?'

'No family.'

'Pity. Lot of it about these days, I mean this not being able to have any . . .'

'Not my fault, dear.'

'*His*.' A nod of the head from Biddulph, a swift 'H'm!'

'Soon be time to go.'

'Know.'

'I brought you this,' and Lil's hand disappeared into the pocket of her two-piece.

'What is it?'

'There,' put the bar of chocolate on the table.

'Ta.'

'They'll let you eat it, I suppose.' Mrs Biddulph cried in her mind, 'innocent', laughed, said, 'Course. They're swine any time, but they have their moments.'

'Warm in this room, isn't it?'

' 'Tis.' A sudden ultimatum, very direct. 'Not worried about the smells *now*?' And a slow shaking of the head from her visitor.

The Biddulph head turned, swiftly raised itself, found the time on the clock, stared at the assembled faces, heard the feet scraping the floor, 'They're ready, Lil, always ready, to bloody rush out of it. Can't blame them of course. Sorry for some kids here, drugs, that sort of thing, silly bitches just the same.' She noticed a restlessness in her visitor, understood, was again abrupt, the words clipped.

'Go if you want.'

'I wasn't thinking of going,' Lil said.

'What else can I say?' thought Lil, took a bold look at the clock. Mrs Biddulph closed her eyes, as if with a sudden disgust.

'But everything went off all right in the end, dear, I mean Mrs Kavanagh and you. You did patch it up.'

'Did.'

'Glad,' Lil said.

'You're glad about a lot of things seems to me, aren't you, dear? Ill in bed she was for a full week, can't think even now how I managed that lot. Got her pension for her. Christ, the fuss about me doing the proxy stuff for her, think I was asking for the Rock of Gibraltar. Fact.' But Lil wasn't listening, hadn't heard a word, but only looking. The worn hand on the next table, palm upwards, motionless, like a surrender, and the owner of it, a tall man, lantern jawed, the look severe from entrance and still severe, the erring daughter under him, the temporary disgrace of a simply ordered, accepted, and contented life. The father who was *right*, warder and judge of the home that he lived in. And at the next table two girls, mouths partly open, holding the All Brite smile, leaning across to the tall blonde, and just listening. They addressed her in unison. And she was all right now then?

'Yes, I'm all right now, ta, but it was that bloody blood really, sight of it, did me proper.'

Lil heard, leapt violently to her feet, rushed to the door, pushed the watcher aside, opened it wide, and seemed to fall into the corridor, before the clock struck, and the iron word would follow after. Hurried to the wall, heaped there, was sick.

*

Back where things were safe, Tench's wife sat up in bed, looked with astonishment at the little blue bedside clock, sighed, got up, and called through the door. 'Luke!' And no answer.

'D'you know what time it is, dear?' And no reply. So louder, the thunderbolt down the stairs, reaching an absorbed man, close under the light.

'It's eleven o'clock, dear.' Though absorbed, he was yet factual, called out in a loud voice, 'Ten past, dear. Won't be long.' He heard the bedroom door slam, after which he continued reading. A world without a calendar, perhaps without clocks. Read.

My dear son,

Have to get this letter off to you, must, *now*, got to. You'd never know how I feel, I mean after last night when my friend and me had a row, terrible, and about you it was, God, she even called me a liar, a *drunken* liar, hypocrite came out in her all of a sudden. Things she *said*.

I cried bitter then, didn't understand, didn't *know*. Was close by her, listened, saw her twice the size you might say. Awful. Was nearly sick, and that on top of not being well. But I do know better than her what it's like when you can't get hold of the stuff. I do hope this letter reaches you, and I'm *still* waiting for that one from you, said you would, know you did, never forget, Sean, never will. Wish I could *push* this letter to you all the way with my own hands, see you get hold of it in yours, open it, read, bring a smile then, your mother's still *there*, waiting, and though it's been a long time and I haven't heard a line, not a single word, it's just the thought that I know you will, and that *you're* there, that's the main thing, knowing it. Ah! I went downstairs last night, and I was real sick, after that look, the bloody words out of my friend's mouth, always so close she was, *so* close, *and* we always understood each other, all along the line we did. She *rushed* out of the house, left me, just left me, banged the door, thought she'd take it off the hinges. I said to myself, and I meant it, 'In the name of Christ, *this* can't surely be true,' never having had a row before, didn't seem real, ah, you'll never properly know, I mean until the lucky day, how I've clung to Lena, her to me. You'd never understand it, son, not while you live. Enough of that for now. Tell me how you are, what's happening, in which sea are you, where are you going to, and what is the name of the next port? And another thing. I'm still waiting for somebody to tell me what M.V. means. I mean *M.V. Devonian*. Did I ever tell you that once I wrote off to some people that call themselves the Angel Line, beautiful name for a line, isn't it? Well, they wrote back saying they had no such ship as the *Devonian*, never had had, so it's the same old thing all over again, and this goes to you care of the GPO, London. One thing I've been meaning to ask you for ages now, is will you send me a photograph of yourself, love that, can't ever remember having a photo of somebody, like some have, stand them on their bedside tables, on a dresser, so you can always look at them, remembering, so that you *never* forget? That's what I want, Sean, my dear son, a really nice photo of yourself. *Do* send. And say something for me, just short'll do, since I always pray for you every single night. I always remember the night I first knew, Lena remembers it, too, a gold evening that was, and if only you'd been *there* at the time. The other day I said to her how I'd like to send a photograph of myself to you, and she laughed in my face saying what nonsense it was, at my age, hear her saying it now, 'Too late for that sort of thing, dear,' she said. I wondered though, not all things are too late. Calls me Brigid, and it's a long, long time since anybody ever called me Biddy which I used to be one time, my father did up to the day he packed up and rushed off to America, lots of people were rushing away then. Not a word to my mother, not a word. Never heard from him again, sort of just got lost in that country. Ah well! The things that happen to people. Only thing I remember about him now is he gave me my first drink of the stuff, first ever, always liked to have it around, he was like that. Do write soon, please, and I mean *please*.

Your fond mother,

Brigid Kavanagh.

The pipe had gone out, and he relit it. He put down the letter, picked up another, a shorter one.

The hand reaching out, all the time reaching out, a life lifted by a thought, the words sustaining, and he knew that there were others like her, hidden away, and that the holes were many.

Dear Sean,

This is only a short letter, was going to be a long one, and then of a sudden it became that sort of evening when a lot of things don't seem to matter to you, don't know why. Couldn't think of anything, didn't want to *do* anything, didn't want to move, just sit here, close my eyes, let the evening just *have* me, that's all. I've said nothing and I want nothing and I don't care nothing. So I just sat, emptied out you might say. Like it most of the evening, even Lena was mystified, couldn't understand it at all, though *I* knew 'cept I just hadn't the word that would say it. *She* calls it having a mood, maybe it is. You feel sort of weary without knowing why, is this all right, is that, how about tomorrow, what's the use, those kind of thoughts in my head and marching about there like little men. Lena went off then, don't know where, didn't ask questions, she's like that sometimes, sort of *leaps* away from you. Remembered to take her shopping bag, never forgets that, and she never returns with it empty. Cute she is, and if she's bent on something you can bet safely that she'll trip into that new place, Soonan's, where they got her once before, like a magnet that shop is, got everything in it you can think of. Call it nicking round here but where they know all about the words they just call it plain stealing. Anyhow, she's gone off, and just at that time of the evening when you have to be *so* careful, have a name for that sort of thing round here, but is only some louts trying to kick your door in, or some silly bitch that's loaded with something she never wanted, and trying so hard to get what she *does*, out of a little needle they always have tucked up their sleeve. So soon's I heard the front door close I rushed downstairs, locked it, and came up again, locked this room door, doesn't pay to forget anything these days, and soon's I heard the click I knew I was safe. If you *did* get that last letter I sent you I hope you'll remember the photo of yourself. Simply love that. Tell you something. It's not often I'm on my own like this, mostly Lena does the writing for me, never very good at writing, but my hand's ready to light on anything at this moment. Wish to God it would land on yours.

Love from your fond mother,

Brigid Kavanagh.

'Demented,' Tench said, dropped the letter, again relit his pipe, and didn't notice how quietly the door had opened, nor see his wife there in her night attire, knew nothing until she spoke.

'Luke! Really! Have you seen what time it is?' He knew. 'Sorry,' he jerked out, picked up the pipe as if to light it again, dropped it, put his hand to the light, switched off, slowly followed her out, closed the door behind him.

'You've got them on the brain,' Vera said, reaching the stairs. He followed after her, feet dragging, they went in, he shut the door.

'Not on the brain,' Tench said.

'What on earth does that mean?'

'Nothing,' he said. 'Doesn't matter.' She returned to bed, turned over, faced the wall, left him standing at a chair, wondering if he would ever begin to undress.

'I'll be glad when this week's over,' she said. He climbed in beside her, and she made to turn quickly, as if to confront and admonish again, but she put out her hand and switched off the light. Feeling her stiffen in the bed, he wondered what might come. Nothing happened, and he turned the other way, watched a wall dissolve into the darkness. He thought of the letters, and he thought of the woman, the very temporary servant of Willesden days. An August morning came clear again, he saw her. In the darkness he hoped that the communion wine was sweet to her.

'Luke.'

'Yes?'

'The children had their light on till nearly ten,' the voice complaining.

'Is that unusual?'

'Had to go in and switch off of course.'

'What was it all about?' he asked.

'Nothing really.'

'Well then. Why the fuss? You switched off?'

'Naturally,' she said.

'Good. Duty done.'

'I've had a beastly headache most of the day,' Vera said. He turned to her. 'Sorry, dear. But you're all right now?'

'I still wish you weren't going to Willesden tomorrow.' And he said nothing.

'I know you're a person that always tries to do the right things, dear.' And after a too noticeable pause Tench said, 'Thank you, dear,' as if the grocer had just handed him a pound of sugar. 'One does one's best, Vera.'

'We all do our best,' she said.

'I'm *tired*,' Tench said, meant it, turned away again, closed his eyes. Her lips at his ear, the final confidence. 'I admire you, dear. I do.'

'Good night,' Tench said.

'Night.'

*

Eddy listened to the first knock, and then to the second.

'God, it's Lil! Course, she's forgotten the bloody key,' and he rushed to the door. 'Lil!'

'Hello,' Lil said, came into the light, and Eddy stared.

'What's the matter?'

'Nothing.'

'*Nothing?* You're as pale as a *sheet*, dear,' led her into the sitting room, sat down beside her, still stared, he had never seen Lil quite like this.

'What happened?'

'Nothing,' Lil said, jumped to her feet, rushed to the bathroom, was sick again, and he behind her, her arms gripped, then holding her head, and crying, 'Nothing, *nothing*, what the hell d'you mean nothing?'

'I'm sorry, Eddy.' And Eddy raged. 'Sorry. Christ! I like that, I really do. You look scared to death and you say nothing happened. It's that damn Good Samaritan business you're on, that's what. Wondered where you'd got to, wondered and wondered, not usual with you to be so late, and to be like *this*,' holding her head, mothering her, angry, sick of the whole business. '*Good* Samaritan,' he said, 'I'm fair sick of the lot of it. Never saw such a change in anybody in a few days.'

'Leave me alone. I'm upset.' Turned to him, 'Can't you *see* I'm upset?'

'I'm not *blind*,' Eddy said. She leaned her weight on him, 'Sad, Eddy, it was *sad*, should've seen what I've seen, what I heard there, and the people, the *people*, and her, Eddy, that poor old woman.' He held her tightly, but he said nothing.

'I'll lie down, Eddy.'

'Course, come on, Lil, let's get you bedded. Come on now,' and helped her to the bedroom, sat her down, 'Half a tick.' She slumped, heard him go out, closed her eyes, wholly unaware that he had returned, was sitting beside her.

'Here, dear,' he said. Her hand shook, and he held the glass to her lips. '*Drink* it, Lil.'

She drank. 'Ugh!' she said.

'That's it, and that's bloody done it,' Eddy said, stood her up, was rough and clumsy in his undressing, nurse-like and comforting when at last she lay, and he stared and stared at the face that was so white, heard her being sick in the bowl again.

'I won't go out this evening.'

'You *must*.'

'And I said I *won't*.'

'Don't be angry, Eddy,' and when she looked up at him he rushed away for a handkerchief.

'Not angry, Lil,' he said, '*not* angry, dear, only worried, whole of this bloody week I'm worried. First you say you don't want to stay here any more and it's mad, I say mad, just because of this bent old woman that should've been in the bin long ago, and now you're doing the Nightingale stuff for this crony of hers. Know where it begun, but how's it going to end, Lil?' and he bent over her, stroked her hair, 'lie in, be quiet, try to forget that bloody place, try to forget everything. I mean that, now. Everything,' crooned in her face, 'poor dear,' sat on the bed, went on stroking her hair. 'There there!' Remembered the week that was good, remembered the week that wasn't. Thought about Betty in Kent, remembered a girl named Ann that would come soon.

'Eddy?'

'What?'

'She cried.'

'*Who* cried?'

'Mrs Biddulph,' Lil said, stroking his hand.

'What . . . *made* you sick?' he asked. And he was as close to her as he had ever been. '*What?*'

'The smell,' she said, 'the smell.'

'Well, my God! You must have been mad, Lil Winten,' paused and then the slow, funereal utterance, 'you know you'll have to be careful, Lil, these old bitches'll have you on the ground if you don't chuck all this. It *is* mad. They're absolute strangers to us, besides which they're not our business, never were. Don't you understand. *Leave* well alone. And that's the end of it, and I'm telling you what it means. End.'

She turned her head away, covered her face with her hands, said quietly, 'Leave me alone now, Eddy,' and he left her alone, and went out, and in the sitting room sat heavily, stared at an empty screen. He thought of tomorrow, the morning time, clapped hands to his head, rocked to and fro on the couch, and always the ear cocked, listening for her call. 'And she'll not go there in the morning, and she'll *not*.'

'Eddy?'

'There!' he exclaimed, and hurried back to her, sat by the bed.

'What, dear?'

'Sit with me, Eddy,' Lil said.

'Course.'

'But don't say anything, don't talk. Just sit there. By me. That's it.'

'How'd you feel?'

'All right now, Eddy,' she said. 'It wasn't anything really 'cept the smell.'

'I won't say anything,' Eddy said, 'not a single word. Just try and get a sleep. Never seen you looking like this, never. So *pale*. God! Thought you'd seen the last ghost when you come in that time.'

'Don't *talk*.'

'No, dear,' feeling for the hand, holding it, it was Lil, she *was* there, real. After a while he heard her gentle snoring.

'Ah! That's better,' and again he thought of the morning. 'Settle everything then. Finish. Had enough, so's she. The bloody interference there is, other people, all the time it's other people. Never let you alone if they can help it. The smell,' he said. 'I wonder what the smell was. Must've been pretty bad to make her sick as a dog. Awful. Should never have gone near the damned place.' He wondered again.

'Prison smell, I suppose.' He looked down at her, was glad she slept, nothing like a good sleep.

'Good job I did decide not to go in this evening. And where'd I have been if it hadn't happened. In The Marquis of course, and yes, if we'd been left a-bloody-lone we'd both have been there.' He bent over her, wanted to say, 'Lil, how are you now?' but refrained, and sat on, her hand in his, heard the snores again. 'Good. Well away.' He heard the clock strike, heard an outside wind, he switched off the light, sat still in the darkness.

'But I won't leave here, not for her or anybody, it's where we are, where we're all right, it's our home. And that's it.' He put an arm across her, he lowered his head, shared a pillow with her, closed his eyes, fell asleep. The night beginning, and for another woman over.

*

'Well now,' Mrs Laurent said, and Mrs Biddulph said nothing. 'I am speaking to you, Mrs Biddulph.'

'I heard.'

'*Well?*'

'Well *what*?' a positive snarl.

'You know you can go.'

'Not that stupid.' Mrs Laurent took an envelope from her pocket, and Biddulph snapped,

'What's that?'

'What d'you think, dear? The money, the *cash*.'

'Her stuff?'

'Yes.'

'Keep it. Told you that three days ago. Didn't know you were deaf.' The well-known room, and fifth down the corridor that always seemed too long, where Kavanagh had so often sat, the 'goodbye' room, from which you walked out into the air, and were free.

'Please take it. You know damned *well* you need it.'

Mrs Biddulph pushed back the envelope, 'And I said what I said,' after which she folded hands in her lap, looked up at the too well-known features. 'I'm going now.'

'I'll send it on to you, nevertheless,' Mrs Laurent said.

'Where to?'

'Wherever you are.'

'Where's that?'

'You'll be somewhere.'

'Always sure, aren't you.' When some tea arrived, Mrs Biddulph accepted it begrudgingly.

'Where are they?' she asked.

'Where are what?'

'Them letters.'

'What letters, dear?'

'She told me day before yesterday, you found them when you were selling out my friend, she told me, where are they?'

'I gave them to a Mr Tench.'

'Who's he when he's around?'

'Mrs Kavanagh once worked for his family, some time ago now, perhaps before you first met her, at midnight wasn't it, when she was flat on the ground. Your own words, dear.' Mrs Laurent stirred her tea, Mrs Biddulph sipped noisily at her own. She put the cup down. 'They're mine. They're mine. My property, you had no bloody right to give them to anybody.'

'They were Mrs Kavanagh's letters, my dear.'

'No. Cod stuff. They're mine, I wrote them, wrote the lot of them.' She leaned forward, put a hand on the Laurent knee, and said loudly,

'He only came out of a cup but was me that kept him

standing up for her. *Me*. Kept her alive, them letters did. You weren't there. Wouldn't bloody know *ever*. Got his breath in her ears, got his hair in her eyes, just think of that. My son as well as hers. Give me the letters.'

'I'll see you get them, I'll send them on to you, dear.'

'No dearie stuff, *please*, and the way you talk, like you knew my every damned step I'm going when I get out of this rotten place, like you knew the door, had the bloody key in your hand, like you knew it all. Where is he?'

'I gather he's the curate at St Jude's,' Mrs Laurent said.

'Where's that?'

'Not far from Totall Point . . .'

Mrs Biddulph spat. '*That* place.'

'Spitting is not allowed here,' Mrs Laurent said. 'Wipe it up.' And she watched the woman bend down and wipe it up. 'You're the most stubborn woman I've ever met in my life. No wonder your family kicked you out.'

'I walked out.'

'You should return to them and say you're sorry. It would do you the world of good, Mrs Biddulph, just to say you were sorry about something.'

'Preaching now.'

'If you are caught at Soonan's again you'll get six months at least.'

'Threatening me now.' Mrs Laurent took the cup from her hand and replaced it on the tray.

'Say thank you.'

'Thank you.'

'That's better. And I'll run you myself to wherever you wish to go.'

'Give me the letters.'

'They're not here. I told you where they were.' Mrs Biddulph was instantly on her feet. 'Then you had no damned right, you hadn't, not your property, was *ours* before she went through that bloody window. How far's St Jude's?'

'Not far.'

'Will you run me to the chap at St Jude's?'

'Come along, Mrs Biddulph, come along, dear.'

'You can keep your damned smile, too.'

'*Come* along now,' and she put a hand behind the woman, ushered her to the door.

'If there's anything at all,' Mrs Laurent said, and immediately the woman beside her said that there wasn't. They reached the door, left the echoes behind them.

'There's my car.' Mrs Biddulph did not reply, allowed herself to be led across the road, in between the knife-like traffic lanes.

'Right,' and she put Mrs Biddulph in the seat beside her. 'I'm sorry for you,' she said.

'Spare the ointment. Where is it?'

'Not far.' The car slackened speed. 'Just around the corner.'

'Don't move, I won't be long,' Mrs Laurent said, left Mrs Biddulph sat staring at the windscreen wiper, it having begun to rain. Tench answered the door. 'Ah! Good morning.'

'Morning, Mr Tench. I've come about those letters you asked for.'

'I thought they were for the rubbish chute,' he said, 'but do come in.'

'Thank you. I shan't keep you long.' He led her to his study. 'I've been reading them,' he said. 'Very interesting indeed.' It sounded like a kick at the door. 'One moment, please,' and left Mrs Laurent standing outside the door, and he had forgotten to offer her a chair. The explosion when he opened the door, was not expected.

'Yes?'

'Your name Tench, Mr Tench?'

'That's right.'

'You've got my letters. I want them.' Tench smiled down at what he saw. 'Do come in, Mrs . . .'

'Biddulph.'

'Mrs Biddulph,' and he led her down the passage.

'That's where you got then,' Biddulph said.

'Do sit down, Mrs Laurent,' Tench said, and he opened the drawer, began gathering the letters together. Mrs Biddulph said, 'I wouldn't have sat down if you'd offered me a chair, which you *didn't*.'

'So sorry, there.' Biddulph stood, Biddulph waited. 'Just the letters. Nothing else.' He bent over her. 'They're your friend's letters, surely?'

'Mine. I wrote them.'

'I don't quite understand. I've read them all, and she signs her name to them.'

'When those letters were writ she didn't know half the time whether she was drunk or sober. Mrs Laurent had no right to give them to you, none of your business, none of it, peeping into what's private, sacred to Brigid they were, don't I know.' And Tench now felt as though he had opened the door to a hurricane.

'Mr Tench, perhaps I should explain. Mrs Biddulph is out today, and the letters are hers, and she wants them back.'

'Certainly,' Tench said, bent over his desk, searching for a big envelope, 'I . . .'

'They were in a *box*. Where's the box?' With a quite pained look Tench looked down at the visitor, and indulging in his most casual manner, said, 'The box was filthy. I threw it away.'

'No bloody right to throw anything away, Mr, wasn't yours to do.' He picked up the sheaf of letters, laid them carefully in the envelope, sealed it, said, 'There, madam. It's this way out.' Biddulph quickly dodged the hand that would lie on her arm, trotted quickly behind the tall man.

'So sorry,' he said.

'Thank you.' Mrs Laurent followed after them. 'Thank you, Mr Tench,' she said, and together they watched the tall, thin woman in the brown coat hurry down the drive to the gate. 'A nice place you have here.'

'Yes, isn't it. Your Mrs Biddulph is a rather angry woman.' He walked with her down the drive.

'She's always angry,' Mrs Laurent said.

'I don't envy you,' Tench said. Mrs Biddulph was stood in the road, facing them both, glaring at them.

'Goodbye, Mrs Laurent, if at any time . . .' the smile following, 'good . . .'

'Come along, dear,' she said.

'I'm not coming anywhere,' Mrs Biddulph said. 'I'm out now, and you can't do the coming on stuff any more. I got what I wanted, and what I didn't want you can do what the bloody hell you like with, so there.' They had crossed the road, and Mrs Laurent had thrown open the door. 'Jump in, dear,' she said, and Biddulph didn't jump.

'You won't take me anywhere,' Mrs Biddulph said.

'Then look after yourself. Perhaps we'll meet again some time, dear, I'm sure.'

'You're always sure, aren't you?'

Mrs Laurent got in and closed the door, gave Mrs Biddulph a parting smile. 'Poor Mrs Biddulph, won't even allow you to be sorry for her,' and watched the woman turn her back, walk quickly down the road, and as she passed her obliged with a final wave of the hand. And the wave stopped Biddulph dead in her tracks. She stood there, glowering, the big envelope tight in her hand, the other clawing air for a moment, then suddenly to her mouth, out of which came two words that were loud in the deserted road. 'I wonder,'

Mrs Biddulph said. She looked back at the rectory, watched a woman arrive at the gate, enter, walk up the drive, saw the big black door opening, the man with red hair come out. 'Ah . . .!' she said, and went off down the road.

'Just had a visitor, dear,' Tench said. 'Two, in fact, *quite* a surprise so early in the morning.'

'Oh yes?'

'There's one of them,' he said, and he pointed to the tall figure now distancing. 'Just let out. Used to live with Mrs Kavanagh. I've never seen such belligerency, such downright anger in anybody.' He seemed on the point of continuing, but Vera slammed shut the door, cut off abruptly what might follow. The hall itself, at this moment, seemed crowded.

'Should have seen the expression on her face when I gave her back the letters,' but Vera was already out of reach, and mounting the stairs. She thought of the children that had gone, and of the Evelyns that would come.

'Where are you?'

'I'm upstairs, dear.'

'Oh yes, of course. All right,' Tench said, disappeared into his study, again, sat down to the new day that was normal.

VIII

Afterwards.

'Seem to remember her, used to wear a big black coat, didn't she?'

'Blue.'

'Black, I know it was.'

'Blue, seen her in it many a time.'

'Perhaps it was sort of blue-black.'

'Maybe.'

'Does it *matter*?'

'*No*.'

'Easy does it, Jack.'

'Well then?'

'Well what?'

'Nothing. Ah! Here she is; evening, Mrs Finch.'

'Good evening.' She unloaded the tray, and from behind the counter, Mr Finch watched.

'I was just saying to Jack here . . .'

'What were you saying?' She did a rapid wipe up around the glasses, removed empty ones.

'He said she used to wear a black coat and I said it was blue.'

'Dead black,' Mrs Finch said, 'and I never once saw it change colour.'

'That's it then.'

'It is.'

'Bottoms up, Jack.'

'Used to sit where you're sitting now,' Mrs Finch said, 'always had that corner, she and her friend. Visitor here long before our time, I believe. They'd have the same thing whenever they came in, never a change. Sometimes I didn't see them for weeks on end.'

'Slack.'

'Not for long. Darts job on tonight, didn't you know?'

'No.'

'They'd come in around eight,' Mrs Finch said, 'never left till closing time. Never spoke much to anybody, the odd hello, good evening. I think they liked minding their own business. They liked the company.' When Jack looked up, she was smiling. 'If anybody laughed, they'd join in. Never any trouble here unless they'd had too much.' And one that could have been Smart Alec's brother piped up with,

'And how about when somebody cried, Mrs Finch?'

'Nobody cries in this house,' she said, 'you've spoken out of turn, and by the way, take your finger out of the beer,' which he did, and sucked it, after which much gurgling.

'Eddy's not in yet.'

'He'll come. Wouldn't miss the darts match for anything.'

'Same again?'

'Right.' Jack marched up to the counter. 'Evening, Mr Finch.'

'Evening,' Finch said, served, and always keeping an eye on the slops. He ignored the proffered smile, glanced at his wife, suddenly remembering. 'Was today, wasn't it, dear?'

'Yes.'

'Poor old thing. That corner'll never seem the same to me somehow. What happened to that friend of hers?'

'Eddy Winten told me she was in again, so he'd heard. She always had more to say than Mrs Kavanagh.'

'Noticed that. God knows how they lived, never seemed to have anything to do.'

'Kavanagh's skivvied around for years, I believe. Know nothing about Mrs Biddulph. They both lived for the bottle and that's the plainest fact of all.'

'True enough. Reminds me, I actually fixed it with Eddy to get a wreath down there, he said Lil was going.'

'Funny, Bill, just thinking of them now. See them come in together, get to that corner, I'd go out to meet them. Usual smiles, and then Kavanagh'd look hard at me, and then at Mrs Biddulph, and then they both looked, and you knew they were waiting for it, and wanting it. Sometimes I used to hate serving them.'

'I'd never have refused them,' Finch said, 'never. Harmless old couple.'

'More harm to themselves, really.' Finch made no reply, surveyed the room. 'Time we were filling up, Cis.'

'Thought the Wintens would have been here by now,' she said, 'what with The Raven lot coming over this evening.'

'Told *me* he was on nights.'

'He'd alter that, 'count of the match. He'd never miss a match.'

'We'll see.'

'Yes.'

She picked up an empty tray, did a brisk run round the room. Jack and Smart Alec indulged in a lively conversation, and she saw this, deliberately avoided the beckoning finger. The clock struck eight. She piled empty glasses into the trough.

'They are late,' she said, began a wash-up.

'Wish he'd collected the wreath, just money wasted,' Finch said.

'Should be here by now, perhaps they're not coming.'

'She wanted him to go with her, but he wouldn't.'

'*What* a mean thing to do.'

'Their business,' he said, again surveyed the room, both

doors. 'And where the hell's Rance got to,' he exclaimed loudly. 'We want at least six dozen Light up here, to say nothing of the Guinness.'

'I'll get it,' Mrs Finch said.

'You can't get it, dear,' Finch replied, nettled, 'where the hell's that basket got to anyhow?' He vanished, leaving her in charge, and she was kept busy, they came up, refilled, went back to their tables, and one cried out, 'No darts?'

'Early yet.'

'Not by my *watch*.'

'Go and sit *down*.' And she sat down, waited for her husband, thought of two that would not come. 'I wonder what she'll do now, expect Probation will do something about it. Very lonely for her now,' and slowly, thoughtfully, 'she's not young.'

'Give's a hand, Cis,' cried Finch, and she rushed to help him, and in the same moment Rance burst in through the door. Finch heaved, sighed, saw him, dropped the case, rushed at him.

'Where the hell have *you* been?'

'Sorry, Mr Finch, something cropped up, missus had to rush away sudden, and then there was a damned hold-up near the crossing.'

'Get cracking.'

'Yes, Mr Finch.'

'Then get hold of the bloody thing,' Finch said, pushed a tray into his hand, and Rance rushed away, hunting for orders, collecting empties.

'I'd slip off now, dear, if I were you,' Finch said, and saw her go behind the red curtains. 'I'll go in later, if there's a chance.'

'You *again*,' Finch said, offered the broadest smile, served him.

'Lost two regulars.'

'We have.'

'Remember that night when the little one complained in a loud voice that you'd given her short measure?'

With a stern look, Finch replied, 'I don't remember.'

'A silly old cow in some ways,' the man said, picked up his glass, went away, and Finch said nothing.

'How about it then?' The shout was so loud, so sudden, Mr Finch sailed from behind his counter, stood four square in the centre of the room, cried, 'What's that?'

'How about it, boss?'

'What?'

'No tele.'

'No tele in this pub on match nights.' Finch went quickly back behind the counter, glanced at his watch, and then the clock. 'Can't understand it, and not even a sight of Eddy. Swore he'd be here for it.' The door opened, Eddy came in.

'There you are.'

'Evening,' Eddy said, looked round for a seat, found full tables, went up to Mr Finch. 'Usual, Bill.'

'Thought you were never coming.'

'Nearly didn't.'

'Anything wrong?'

'Nothing.'

Finch served. 'The Raven lot haven't shown up yet, and loud mouth Crickle's been crying for the tele. Know why?'

'Nipple night,' Eddy said, without smiling.

'Night of the tits has gone flat for once. Dirty old bugger,' Finch said, remembering a previous Friday, a splendid pair of them, and a smile like an hurrah behind, and the slack wet mouth, the smile still spilling. Remembered looking across his counter at eyes fish open, the gawping assembly. He looked up suddenly. 'You go?'

'No, I didn't,' and at once Finch knew that Eddy Winten was in on a mood. 'Seat over there, Eddy.'

'Ta,' and Eddy went to it and sat down, his back to the counter, and ran his finger round the tip of the glass. 'Shouldn't have come at all. Why did I?' He poured down the ale. 'Never had such a bloody week in all my life,' and when suddenly he looked up Finch was there, a dragged chair behind him. 'Move in, Eddy.' Eddy sat up, stiff, said abruptly, 'Had a bloody 'nough of it for one day,' finished off his drink.

'Same again?'

'In a minute,' Eddy said.

'Can see you're upset.'

'Telling me. What a mess.' Finch picked up the glass, went away and refilled it, came back.

'On me.'

'Thanks, Bill.' He had never seen Eddy so nervy, so tense. And in a flash, knew.

'All that bloody way to Willesden, awful journey she had, and when she got there seemed to be nobody around at all.'

'Reminds me, I forgot the wreath.' Eddy was curt, said, 'Doesn't matter, does it?' picked up the glass.

'Good health, Mr Finch,' and Finch raised his own.

'Bad business all round, Eddy, was quick to see how the missus noticed when she went out to serve this evening.'

'Ah!'

'Lil's not coming in then?'

'No. Wouldn't let her. Bad enough the way she's been since it happened, hates where we are now, wants us to get out of it, how the hell can you get out of anything now, everybody hanging around these days, just waiting for the word go, few black faces as well. We were quite happy there till this lot happened.' He suddenly gripped Finch's sleeve, 'Tell you something,' and the voice dropped, and Eddy peered round the room, 'actually found my wife standing by the bloody window as if she wanted to go, too. Scared the lights out of me.'

'Like this window-ledge stuff,' Finch said, '*never* seen so many lunatics around as there are today,' and he covered Eddy's hand. 'All over now, Eddy, few days everything will be back where it was. People soon forget. Good thing in some ways.' Eddy was close again, and Finch bent to listen.

'Everything's been all over the place since last week, and only yesterday she came home sick's a dog, vomiting all over the place she was, been to see the other old one stuck in Holloway. What a lark.' His finger stabbed the table. 'Charitable's the next man, you know that, Bill?' Bill nodded. 'But God Almighty you can't go on being sorry for somebody *all* the time, well can you, got to be ended sooner or later. All that stuff in only one week, like a bloody year to me.'

Mr Finch put a hand on Eddy's shoulder. 'Could see you were upset soon's you came in the door. Never mind, it's not the end of the world. Here! Sup that up and have another.'

'Course I'm upset.'

'Eddy?'

'*What?*'

'I think you ought to go home, lad,' Finch said.

'Think I ought.'

'You *do* that. Never seen you like this before. Come along now,' and he got Eddy on his feet. They went to the counter. 'Wait,' Finch said. Eddy waited. He watched him wrap up a small flask in coloured paper, turn, offer the bottle.

'What's this?'

'Take it back for Lil. Tell her I was asking about her, and we hope to see you soon. Place isn't the same without you,' and he pushed the small parcel into Eddy's pocket.

'Rather pay.'

'Take it.'

'Thanks.'

The door burst open, The Raven crowd flooded in, rushed for the counter. Mr Finch followed Eddy to the door, caught the air in his face, liked it. 'I didn't feel too good. Perhaps I shouldn't have come.'

'Go *home*.'

'Night. Thanks again.'

'Night,' Finch said, caught his wife's eye, hurried back.

'You can slip in now, dear,' she said, 'it's all ready on the table.'

'Right, dear. Keep Rance on his toes, won't you?'

'I will.'

'Eddy Winten dropped in, didn't stay. Never seen him so upset.'

'She all right?'

'Had one hell of a day down Willesden way he reckons. Oddest funeral she'd ever been to she told him. Way he told it it *did* seem odd, only wanted the box to be missing to make it a day.'

'It'll be cold, dear,' Mrs Finch said, gently pushed him behind the curtain.

'Mrs Finch.' She turned, recognized the woman at once. 'Well! Evening, Mrs Laurent.'

'Won't keep you a second,' Mrs Laurent said, opened her bag, fished about inside, whilst Mrs Finch wondered what might come out of it.

'Doubt if you'll be calling here again,' Mrs Finch said.

'I doubt it, too. I was on my way home, thought I'd leave this. Perhaps if Mrs Biddulph drops in you'd give it her. She'll need it, few pounds from Mrs Kavanagh's belongings. When I went to see her the other day she positively refused it. I'm sure you can do the trick.'

'If she comes, yes,' Mrs Finch said, and put the envelope

between the bottles on the shelf. 'Somehow or other, I've a feeling I won't see her again.'

'I think you will,' Mrs Laurent said, 'she'll need the company. You rarely get away from what you're used to.'

'I'd never be sure about that,' replied Mrs Finch.

'Good night, and thank you.'

'Welcome,' and then ran after her. 'A moment.'

'Yes?'

'How can I give it to her if she's "in"?'

'She's not "in", she's out, and I'm sure she'll look in on you.'

'Right.' Finch came in after a hasty supper. 'Who was that you were talking to?'

'Never guess. That Mrs Laurent. Brought this envelope for Mrs Biddulph,' and she pointed to the envelope between the bottles. 'Cash for her.'

'I see. Time we were tuning up, dear,' he said, went down the room, got lost in the crowd, pushed through, inspected the dart board.

'Begin.'

*

Eddy stood outside the pub, seemed uncertain about which way he should go. Put the question, and got the answer.

'Would you have enjoyed the match? No. You wouldn't.' He turned the corner, walked leisurely back to Totall Point.

'Eddy,' Lil said, hearing the key turn in the lock. He came in.

'What happened?'

'Changed my mind,' he said, 'just didn't feel like it, Finch was disappointed.'

'But you love playing,' Lil said.

'Said I changed my mind,' Eddy replied, sat down beside her.

'Be glad when this day's over,' she said.

'Listen who's talking.'

'Wish you *had* come,' she said. 'Complete stranger there. Felt so out of it.'

'Done, isn't it. All that matters.'

'Asked me how I liked living tall, knew what he meant, so I said I've been tall so long that all I can say is "how's things down here?" Made him laugh. Funny chap he was.'

'What the hell are you talking about?' and his hand went to his pocket for the flask, and then withdrew.

'Undertaker chap, Eddy, told you, name was Breezeby. My only laugh in the book was when he offered to run me back here in what he'd got.'

'Did he now? Very funny indeed,' Eddy said. 'Ha, ha, ha, bloody ha.' Again his hand went to his pocket, hesitated.

'Eddy?'

'Well?'

'Glad I did go though, even though I was confused all the time I was there, even when he give me a bit of soil, said, "*throw* it, dear," and I threw it.'

'Helmet there?'

'Just this priest chap, and Breezeby, and one other chap that hardly spoke, knew by his gob he was council. God! The way it *blew*. And what a place! Huge!'

'Was a suicide, was public,' Eddy said. 'Remember that helmet hanging round here for nearly three days. Why I mentioned it.'

'Leastways it was quiet and private, all the way back I was glad I'd done it. Can't get Mrs Biddulph out of my head.'

He stared at her, but said nothing.

'Sorry you missed the match, Eddy.'

'Doesn't matter.'

'But I *am*,' she said, 'know you like dart matches there.'

'Doesn't . . . *matter*.'

'I'll make a cup of tea,' Lil said, and when she got up he pulled her down again.

'Half a minute,' he said, and out came the flask in its coloured paper. 'Here. Present for you from Mr Finch. Decent of him, I thought. Doubt if I'd ever frequent any other pub now. *Take* it.'

'Brandy! Well! That's a treat, hope you thanked him proper.'

'What d'you think I am? Give it here. Don't bother about the tea.'

'I'll get them,' she said.

'Stay put,' and he went off to the kitchen and returned with two glasses. 'There! And good luck, and everything,' he said, drank.

'You're still the best husband a woman ever had,' and she gave him a smile. 'You still don't mind Ann coming here?'

'No.'

'Fancy meeting her on the embankment of all places,' Lil said. 'I am looking forward to seeing her.' Eddy smacked his lips, and said, 'Good.' He got up, switched on the tele. 'Wonder what's on?' waited, got the picture, changed channels. 'Ah! Not much, really. Why'd they always put on the posh stuff this time of night,' and he switched off.

'Nothing at all then?'

'Nothing,' and he sat down again.

'Another, Eddy?'

'No. Going to bed,' he said, and left the room. 'Don't be long.'

'Shan't.'

The door banged. He began to undress. It was over, done with, and he felt relieved about it. 'Are you coming, Lil?' He heard a key turn in the lock, a bolt shot home. He was in bed when she came in. He watched her undress.

'She's still got that bloody night on the brain,' he thought.

And as she climbed in beside him he turned his face to the wall.

'Eddy?'

'I'm *tired.*'

'I know you are, and you've been very good, Eddy. But you always are,' she said, turned to him, and he faced her.

'No more nonsense,' he said.

'What d'you mean?'

'You got those two old women off your back. Good. I've had enough. Okay? So it's how about *us*? This is where *we* live. *Our* lives, not theirs, ever since that bloody night you're a changed woman, Lil.'

'What night?'

'*That* night.'

'You make it sound like a *sin*, Eddy.'

'Come here,' and he hugged her. 'Last week I felt safe, and now I'm not. Savvy? All this damned nonsense about pulling out of here.'

'Sorry I spoke.'

'But you *did*, didn't you? Never left the bloody thing alone.' He knew she was angry, knew she was tired, after the Willesden day.

'The Tomsons are leaving,' she said.

'*Let* them.'

'Strange with the next door one empty.'

'Somebody coming in. Let's hope it's somebody different from the last lot.'

'I'll never mention them again.'

'*Good.*' He switched out the light, lay staring at the window.

'Night.'

'Night, Eddy.' He buried his head in the sheets. The Finch words got under, too, reached him.

'Lot of it about these days, Eddy, people standing on

rooftops, hanging on ledges, plain balmy, seems to get some people.' Her restlessness irritated him. 'Can't you settle down? Sleep?' But she was close again, crying quietly, and he thought, 'Christ! She'll have me nuts.' He cursed inwardly as he soothed. 'There there! All over now.'

'I'm all right now,' she said, and he said nothing, again turned his face to the wall.

'Won't be satisfied till she has me out of here,' he thought, still close to open windows, dizzying ledges, rooftops. Wants a bloody good talking-to. I'll see that chap Moore, bring him here.' He half sat up, leaned across, whispered, 'You all right?' And she was, fast asleep.

'Thank God for that.'

IX

THE road was long, and she was still walking, it might have no end, but this was the thing to do. She saw nothing, and heard nothing, and she kept the big white envelope tight under her arm. She halted.

'I'm tired,' and she looked back the way she had come, at last saw things, heard voices round her. 'I'll sit here,' and sat, watched a river.

'Wish I'd gone now.' She lay the envelope on her knee, her hands pressed upon it.

'Nice to sit down,' and she closed her eyes, enjoyed the ease of the moment, opened them again, and the river was still flowing by.

'Strange I'm here, and she isn't. Poor dear. Wish to God I'd gone.' The very feel of the paper made her remember 'the bitch', hating the tall man with red hair, 'Reading my bloody letters, the damned cheek. My letters. *Mine*. Written for her, every Wednesday I wrote them for her.' A bus roared by, a clock struck, children's voices hit the air.

'Nice. So quiet here.' River vanished, and sounds ceased. There was only a woman flat on her back, in a gutter, the road deserted, yellowish light from a lamp. Bending down, looking at her, a face in the rain. 'What on earth are you doing here, dear, know what time it is? It's *raining*. Get up.' Helping her up, holding her, staring at her. 'Where you going?'

'What time is it?' The sudden swaying, even more sudden smell. 'You're drunk, dear.'

'Am I?'

'Yes. Where you from?'

'Willesden.'

'Willesden. What you doing here, dear?' She didn't know, not yet, and Mrs Biddulph put a hand through her arm, 'Let's get out of this anyhow,' leaving the gutter behind, walking her slowly along, leaning her against the wall, again staring at her. 'Old woman.'

'Say you come from Willesden. To here?'

'I walked from Willesden, and then I lost my way, and then I went into a pub. What time is it now?'

'Come along, dear,' Mrs Biddulph said. 'You are a one I must say.' Their footsteps rang out in the deserted road.

'Well! This is a real do, isn't it? Where'd you live, dear?'

'Where am I?'

'Shan't be long now, dear.'

Getting her home, 'walking all that way, from Willesden.' Opening a door, pushing her in, closing and locking the door, taking her into the light, seeing her for the first time. 'Oh dear!' Mrs Biddulph said, sitting her down, holding her as she swayed, the eyes blinking at her, 'must be seventy if she's a day.'

'Lie back. That's right. You'll be okay in a minute. I'll make tea.'

'She's Irish, but what on earth's she doing round here, miles away from Willesden?' making tea, returning to the tiny sitting room.

'Here, come over here, better. Can fall asleep in that armchair if you want to. You do look tired, dear. D'you take sugar?' Swaying again, making her comfortable, laying back the head, removing the hat, opening the big black coat. 'There! Sit up now. Here's your tea.' Watching her drink, then holding her shaking hand, 'Drink it up. That's right. What you want is a good night's sleep. You can tell me all about yourself in the morning.'

'Must have friends here, perhaps she once lived here,' taking the cup, standing her up, removing the coat. 'You can have this couch, not much but I think you'll snore on it,' removing outdoor things, laying her back, when she immediately turned over on her face, said, 'Oh dear! Ah! That's better,' a hand out, offering it to the woman standing over her, as though to say, 'Please take it.'

'Thank you,' she said, feeling the Biddulph hand.

'Tell me all about it tomorrow,' Mrs Biddulph said.

*

And a voice in her ear, softly, 'Are you all right, madam?' Opening her eyes again, feeling the paper on her knee, looking up, a policeman there, not noticing his concerned look.

'Oh!' she exclaimed. His arm came down, his hand gripped the bench. 'Been watching you.'

'Have you?'

'Yes. I wondered how long you were going to sit there,' he said.

'I'm all right,' Mrs Biddulph said, 'just stopped for a sit down.'

'Not ill?'

'Not ill.'

'Good. But don't sit here too long, madam, it's always a little chilly by the river.'

'I'm all right.'

'You said you were. But don't stay too long.'

'I won't stay too long. My friend's gone into the dark.'

'Has she? And left you sitting in the light.'

'That's right.'

'Won't forget what I said?'

'I won't forget.'

'Good,' and he turned and walked away, turned again, threw her a little smile, 'don't catch cold now.' She called to him as he went, 'Thank you,' but he didn't hear, and walked into the distance.

'Some of them are nice, when they remember, half of them don't. That's the trouble. Fancy me seeing Brigid like that, *now*, of all times, must have dropped off, dreamed it. I'd better get on,' and didn't, and held up the envelope, began to open it, dropped it into her lap.

'Can't. Not really. But they *are* mine,' suddenly looking to right and left of her, as if someone might pounce, steal them. 'Poor Brigid.' The policeman forgotten, a striking clock unheard, the moments coming up. A night's chill followed by morning damp, coming into a room, and a heap in the chair.

'You asleep, dear?' Looking at her, the loose, aimless hands, the head low on the breast, and very still. Leaning in to her.

'You all right, dear? Are you awake,' a hand on the arm, feeling it, 'did you have a good night?' The head moving, the eyes opening, a bewildered look.

'Where am I?' Bending low, and saying, 'You're here, dear, you're just here. This is where *I* live. How'd you feel? Thought I'd never get you back last night, really didn't, you were as drunk as a lord. Yes, dear. You were,' and the first Biddulphian laugh, the loose hands caught and held. 'Glad you had a good night. You'll have to tell me all about yourself when we've had some breakfast.'

'You haven't, I mean . . .' Mrs Biddulph knew. 'No, dear, we haven't. Not at the moment. But we'll see about it. I *do* understand.'

'Thank you, very kind of you. I was really lost last night.'

'Must've been mad, walking all that way. Willesden. *Miles* away.'

'Threw me out.'

'Who threw you out?'

'Parson man.'

'Parson?'

'Mr Tench.'

'Who's he when he's out?' A Kavanagh finger beckoned, she bent over her, 'Yes?' And a whisper barely heard, 'Doesn't matter.'

'Wandering in her mind a bit, I'm sure,' thought Mrs Biddulph, and asked very directly, 'Where do you live, dear?'

'Nowhere.'

'Nowhere?'

'I don't understand.'

'Doesn't matter. Worked for everybody one time, used to be in kitchens all over London, once worked in a big house, don't now, retired.'

'How'd you live?'

'Pension.'

'Oh! I'm pension, too. I don't work anywhere either. What'll you do?'

'Nothing.'

'Must do something, dear,' Mrs Biddulph said.

'I sit around, I wait, when the pubs open I go in. It's all right then.'

'What about your *people*?'

'Haven't any. Long time ago that, doesn't matter very much to me. Where do you live?'

'Here.'

'Your house?'

'Rented. Council. Falling to pieces, really, they didn't seem to mind the rats, neither did I. Roof over your head. That's it.'

'Where's your lot?'

'Leeds.'

'Where's that?'

'Yorkshire.'

'What are you doing here then?'

'Living.'

'And you like it?'

'Better than nothing,' and then the salvo. 'You didn't have any place to go last night, you didn't know where you were walking to, or what for or why seems to me, and I knew you were a one that liked to be close to a bottle, so do I. Stay here if you want to. How'd you feel?'

'I'm beginning to feel all right now,' Mrs Kavanagh said.

'That's better. I wouldn't ever go back to Leeds if you give me a fortune. Had that. Like being myself now, not bits of other bloody people that's what I was up there, mean bitch of a daughter I had, got the word scoot in my ear soon's she told me she was getting spliced. I'm on my own now, and I like being here, and I always try hard to keep out of everybody's way and that's my damned ticket, Mrs. Stay here if you want to, only if you want to, pay half the rent and that. That's if you really haven't *got* a place, and you like to be in somewhere. How old are you, dear?'

'Sixty,' Mrs Kavanagh said, 'and thank you very much. I'll do my stuff next Wednesday.'

'What's Wednesday?'

'Pension day.'

'Mine's Friday.'

'If the pub's there I'm all right, I *really* am, though sometimes things happen, I mean I've been in and out for years, got used to it now, like having two homes.'

'Plain drunk?'

'That's right. But cheery with it,' Mrs Kavanagh said.

'You didn't mind what I just said, I hope you didn't, leastways . . .'

'Leastways what, dear?'

'You're not shocked with me being in and out all the time. If you were I'd have to go away, course you get used to almost everything, don't you. *I* do.' Mrs Biddulph laughed. 'We're a pair, dear. I like lifting things sometimes, only sometimes, wouldn't make a habit of it, you know, but if the thing's there, you just can't help it. Sometimes it's a bottle, sometimes it's something I fancy. I've been in a few times myself.'

'I never did mind putting up with things, Mrs . . .'

'Name's Lena, dear. Do remember.'

'As I was saying,' and a sudden burst, 'oh, but I am glad I met you, I really am, you wouldn't believe it, mostly I shy away from people.'

'Have you any things, dear?'

'What things?'

'Just things?'

'What I'm in,' Mrs Kavanagh said, and Mrs Biddulph said, 'Oh! That all then?'

'That's all, Lena, you don't mind, I mean you wouldn't change your mind, I'd only have to go away then, and though I'm used to the going away business most of the time, it'd be nice not to have to now and again.'

'Said we're a pair, didn't I?'

'So you did . . .'

'Lena, dear. *Lena.*'

'Thank you. That's it, Lena. *So* glad I met you last night.'

'That's all right then,' Mrs Biddulph said.

'Tell you more,' Mrs Kavanagh said. 'Never ask questions, so I don't have to look for answers, keep to myself, like you, keep out of the way, that's the thing, bothering nobody, being left alone's nice.'

'Nobody'll bother you here.'

'Say good morning if you're spoke to,' Mrs Biddulph said.

'If I want to, yes, but if I don't, I won't. I'm like that.'

'Soon's I wake up in the morning I know what to do with the time.'

'Do you?'

'Yes, I kill it,' Mrs Biddulph said.

'Sometimes I like sitting in the park.'

'So do I?'

'I used to go and sit in a big library once, but not now, last time they said I was talking to myself and they had me out, full of old men the place was, bits of glass in their hands, reading the newspapers.'

'It's warm there sometimes, especially if it's winter time.'

'Told you we're a pair.'

*

The envelope fell from her knee with a soft thud, and then the man's voice in her ear, 'Excuse me, madam, you dropped this.' Looking up, seeing him, tall, close, and a stuttered exclamation.

'Oh! Thank you, thank you very much.'

A smile in her face, the words closer. 'Forty winks, dear, yes?'

Watching him go, holding on to the envelope, listening to the silence, trying to remember where she was, and all that water still flowing by.

'Things that come into your head when you're sitting nice and peaceful. How long have I been here? Where was I going? Of *course*, that's it,' alert, sitting up, looking around. 'Came away from there, must be a clock somewhere, sure I heard one strike before.' Rising, walking up and down, the bench length, sitting again.

'He said it was chilly here, I haven't noticed, fancy a

policeman smiling at you, walking away like that, not caring, I suppose, and the thing he didn't say, so unusual,' the words ringing in her ear, 'Move along now.'

Rising again, sitting down, 'If I get up I'll just go. Where?' And saw him come back, right back, and hurriedly rose and walked away, back by the way she had come, hurrying, and not knowing why, wondering, and getting no answer, then he passing her, stopping to look, catching her by the arm, another generous smile.

'I wondered when you'd go. It has gone really chilly, madam, have you far to go?'

'Not far.'

'That's good.'

'Suppose it is.'

'Morning.'

'Morning, sir,' halting again. 'First time I ever said "sir" to one of them, probably never even heard. I'd better keep on going, yes, that's it, keeping on going,' the letters under the arm, pressing them tight, wondering why she did. 'Should've thrown them in the bloody river, lot of rubbish, doesn't mean anything now, *nothing*, what'll I do after I pitch them in, what?' The word in her ear, big as a fist. '*What?*'

'Where am I walking to?' And another bench, green, inviting, wanting to sit again, and going on, and on, 'God! This is the longest bloody road I've ever been in.' She dropped the envelope again, had to, her hands to her ears, keeping the words out, didn't mean anything, then, now, keeping them out.

'Yesterday,' she muttered, 'yesterday.' And the words again, at last, remembering yesterday, big man, soft voice stroking moustaches, holding her with an eye, speaking.

'You may go. You are discharged.' Again a bench, sitting on it, a clenched fist, hammering it on her knee. 'Bloody rubbish, I'll throw it in, I will,' rushing to the wall, holding it aloft, a mother and child watching, and then in a loud voice, 'No, I bloody won't,' and turning away, beginning to run, running, a mother watching.

'What a silly woman, dear, isn't she?' The child laughed her out into the distance.

'Come along, dear,' mother said.

*

'If I went down there I could go in, get a cup of tea. Think about things.' Which things?

'Soon be afternoon, any afternoon'll do, they're all the same.' Walking again, the thing to do, if you don't go on walking you don't get the answer.

'She could be quite stupid, poor dear, mercy she never really knew,' a morning rising high, and words falling down the stairs.

'Lena?'

'Well?'

'It's this wireless.'

'What about it, dear?'

'Won't go.'

' "Oh God!" and I actually remember saying it, out loud, she must've wondered at the time, "bring it down, let's see about it." Awkwardly down the stairs, sitting on the bottom one, a small radio set in her hands. "Thought I'd take it to Deveney, he's good at it." '

'Take it.' A whole morning of it, trying to find the world. Not finding it.

'There you are. I thought you'd really done the bunk.'

'Been everywhere with it,' Mrs Kavanagh said, 'they all laughed.'

'Not surprised, that set came out of the ark, dear.'

'I did get voices on it once.'

'Ghost ones, I dare say. It's what they said it was. Bloody rubbish. Chuck it away. What d'you want the damned thing for anyhow? Music?'

'No harm trying,' Mrs Kavanagh said. 'You're not angry with me, are you?'

'No harm not trying neither. The bin's just outside the window, dear.' And she felt it, a tiny little laugh inside her. She picked up the envelope, held it close to her eyes, for the first time read.

'Letters. Brigid Kavanagh.'

'Just fancy me remembering that morning, so real,' all other mornings ruthlessly killed. 'When I think about it now, all the bloody fuss about an old wireless, silly old woman, *voices* inside it!' deprecatingly, 'in the end she was so close to the one thing all the time was hard to know whether she was with the light or she wasn't.' Mrs Biddulph laughed to herself, 'Believed in everything, that woman, everything, I'd say to her when she looked far away, "Anything wrong?" she'd say. "No," I'd say. "I'm glad, dear, just wondered, look on your face has got years in it. Savvy?" "H'm!" She never did savvy somehow. Funny the way she used to say, "Just waiting for the light, Lena, the light." '

*

Two men together, one smirking, one smiling.

'Talking to herself,' one said.

'Let them out early in the morning now, how things are changing, one time had them behind bars. Look at her, and actually laughing now.'

'Pandora's box on her knee no less,' the other said, 'let's,' and they hurried quickly on, and very anxious that a lone woman should be left quite alone on a sea of road, lost in her own thoughts. And only a passing motorist saw a tall thin woman get up from a green bench, walk to the wall, hurl a big white envelope into the river, lean there, watching it drift away, and the days with it.

'Glad I done it. Glad. Finished.' The footsteps in her ears, a man walking by, turning sharply, pouncing, stabbing words into the air.

'What is the time, sir?'

'Dinner time.'

'I'm sure there used to be a big clock round here one time, I often heard it strike . . .'

'Isn't.'

Gone. And she looked up the road, down the road, manless. Leaning on the wall again, talking to the water.

'I'd like to hide somewhere, just for a little while.' Feeling the cold stone under her hand, a sudden glitter in her eye.

'Wish I could walk away from myself for a bit, that'd be nice, just thinking about it, wish I could.' Don't stay, don't wait, nothing in it, nothing, get up, go, go where?

'Ah! Wish to Christ it'd never happened, been with her now, silly old thing she was sometimes, real silly, I didn't mind, you don't really, get used to anything in time.' He was there, quick as light, out of the blue, towering, studying her.

'You still here, madam, I thought I told you to get along,' leaning back, rocking a little, 'course, you are the same person, saw you, you been on that bench a long time, madam, you'll stick to it altogether if you don't watch out. You *look* cold, and I did tell you, well, didn't I? Not the place for an old lady like you, not this time of the year, now why don't you just go on home? Up you get, that's it, all right, that's all right then,' a slight push, 'and do hurry, madam, could rain any minute,' a fugitive look upwards, 'might even snow, you wouldn't like that at all. You are all right?'

'Said I was all right before.'

'Say it now.'

'I'm all *right*,' Mrs Biddulph said. So he half bent, was close to her, saw the years, the tiredness in them, was firm, final.

'Then get *along*, dear.'

'I am,' Mrs Biddulph said. She rose, shook herself, stiffened, brushed herself down.

'Glad it's done. If you stay here much longer that river'll start flowing the other way, bring that stuff back, awful, and the days with it. No. Don't *want* them.' He watched her go, sat quietly down on the vacated bench, looked at a watch, looked further, and she was moving, at last, bent and moving.

'Sort of got herself lost, they do sometimes,' getting up, striding on, hands behind his back, facing the world, never turning to see her as she went, as she again wondered where this road might end.

'*Must* have dozed off, must.'

'Ah!' she exclaimed, halted. The end of the road, looked ahead, saw three more roads eating each other. Crossed one, a sharp look right and left, the word 'Café' large in her eye. And Lena paused at the door, talked to Lena.

'Go in.'

'Yes. All right. I will,' going in, a bell ringing, some people seated, one reading, one staring out of the window, sitting down, a waitress there like magic.

'Yes?'

'Tea, please.'

'Pot?'

'Cup.'

'Anything with it?'

'No,' not looking at her, not seeing her go, beyond the mutterings at the exit. 'Don't touch written all over that one,' the waitress said, descending stairs. Mrs Biddulph sat still, saw no one, stared at a soiled cloth, cheap cardboard crying, 'Today's Menu.' The waitress came.

'Three pence.'

Watching a purse come, a hand as claw, clutching, then searching, finding the coins, paying.

'Ta.' The clock said twelve, had no tick, she stirred tea in a cup, sipped.

'Nice and hot.'

Tealeaves in the cup, whirring them round with a spoon, nothing coming up, nothing to light it up, drinking again, then a furtive look round, at people, things, a clock with one hand, a waitress at the end of the room, waiting, the bell ringing again, she darting forward, the usual stuff, mercenary smile.

'Yes.'

' 'Nother cup please,' Mrs Biddulph called.

'Thank you.'

'Sure you don't want anything with it?' hovering.

'Said no, didn't I?' Looking up, and stare for stare. 'And don't you stare at me.'

'Wasn't.'

'I'm glad,' and loud enough for curiosity, people looking up, at her, old woman, lot of them about these days, forgetting her. She got up.

'You haven't paid for the second cup.' More delving, finding, 'Here! Bloody awful tea you make, how on earth d'you manage it?' right into the waitress's face, rushing to the door, tearing it open, banging it shut.

'Damn everybody!' Leaning against a lamp, closing her eyes, getting bearings again. Opening them, looking at the sky. 'Helmet said it'd rain, and it hasn't, moving off, another road beckoning, walking along. The hand in the pocket, the purse there, feeling it, fishing, where are they? Halting on a corner, taking it out, opening it, the coins out, counting them. 'They'll be open.' Increasing her pace, looking for the sign, suddenly remembering The Marquis.

'Not *there*?' No. All the things too close.

'Here we are.'

'The Eagle.' The big door thrown wide on to the road, like a smile, a voice saying 'come in'.

'Gin, please. Have you any hot water?'

'Ah!'

'Looks like rain,' the man said, a ghost voice in her ears.

'Yes,' gulped out. 'Somebody told me it might snow.'

'Might.'

'Please.' Hands on the table, waiting for him. Feeling the glass in her hand.

'That the hottest water you got?'

' 'Fraid it is.'

'Doesn't matter.'

'You forgot to pay.'

'Sorry.' She moved, jerking from one side to the other, he watched from behind the counter, saw a black hat, a long coat, watched skirting of it flap as she moved.

'You Okay?'

'I'm fine. How are you?'

'I'm fine, too,' and the laugh to follow.

'Your pub's empty.'

'Fills up around one, not much business these days,' ending it, turning his back on her, forgetting her, rearranging bottles on a shelf.

'Another.'

'Coming, madam.'

'Wait!' and he waited. The coins spilled from the purse he caught one as it rolled clear, watched her gather them, count, 'Oh Christ!' Mrs Biddulph said, looked, '*Two* short,' she said.

'Doesn't matter. There you are,' a waved hand, back to

the bottles. Polishing he said, 'Tramp. Lots about these days,' looked forward any moment now to known faces, known hailings, the place filling up. Through the mirror saw her rise, push her way clear. He did not turn.

'Morning.'

He did not answer, and he did not turn. She stood on another corner.

Promptings.

'Say it.'

'Say what?'

'What you want to say, what you *must*.'

'I'm going now.'

'You said that before.'

'Saying it again, got to go.'

'Where?'

'Anywhere.'

'You should have *gone*.'

'I know.'

'At the least, *cried*.' Smoke in her eyes. 'You all right, lady?'

'I'm fine,' Mrs Biddulph said.

'It would have helped you know.'

'I know.'

'Cry then, *cry*.'

She walked round the corner, soiled handkerchief to her face, crying, remembering, knowing. 'Should've, *should've*, wish to Christ I had.' The moments rising again, smothering them, the voice in her ears.

'It's no use.'

'I know it isn't.'

'What'll you do?' And the long wait, and the emptiness, the lips parting, closing, parting again. 'Nothing.'

'Perhaps that's best.'

'Perhaps it is.'

'I always remember the night her son was born.'

'So do I. Was there, heard, know all about that.'

'She said, she said . . .'

'Yes?'

'She said, "You're the best friend I ever had, the best best friend, and if I ever thought I'd wake up and you weren't there, there'd be nothing after that." '

'Sounds as if she meant it, dear.'

'She did. Sometimes, I mean during all this morning, I've felt her hand top of mine, like it was yesterday again, and the other days, and everything as it used to be.'

'You did once curse her, and her paper son, you were pretty drunk yourself that night, remember, number five Gag Lane and the doors locked, the fire there was always nice, specially in the evening time, you'd be very close them times, not a pub in London open, and not *really* wanting you if they were. The light in the bottle always set fire to the tea. That was good.'

'Said she'd die drunk.'

'Know that.'

'Nothing to drink in Willesden.'

'Not now.'

'Makes you think.'

'It does indeed.'

'If you have nothing to lean on you sort of remember what's warm in "hello", even warmer in a nice "good morning". Being wanted's the thing.'

'Found that out three times this morning, in different places. It'll soon be evening. I might know what to do then.'

'You might indeed. It's the waiting, really, the bloody waiting, not everybody understands what that word *means*.'

'I'd say that was *very* right.'

'And glad you think so.'

'Didn't she once say that she liked sitting in pubs, watching people living?'

'Something like that.'

'Nice.'

'We were quite all right one time.'

'You're not now, that's the difference. And you'll still have to wait, think about everything, when you're near to the end of something that's the time you have to be *very* careful.'

'Yes.'

'Know what I *won't* do.'

'What?'

'Go North.'

'A bloody long way that, and they say it's nearly always snowing.'

'And hadn't you better start walking again, you've had your little cry, and I'm sure it's done you good, good for everybody, a bit of a cry, shifts the weight, the feel of it, even the very thought of it.'

'I'm going.'

'Then *go*.' Walking again, another road, how many roads, roads all over the place, a sudden halt, staring round.

'What is this place? Where am I?' It stared down at her, it went on staring.

'Christ! Look where I *am*,' turning away, walking quickly, not looking back, not wanting to, crying in her mind, 'that bloody cursed place,' the smothering mass, that Totall bloody Point that had been so total. Another bench, painted brown, solid as rock, under the height.

'I'm tired, I really am.' Running a hand slowly along the bench. 'Of course, we sat here one night, remember now, we'd just got back, hear her now, saying it, "*Do* come up, Lena, lonely up there, oh how I wish you'd move in with me, I do wish that." '

'Strange, it was dark then, very dark, remember that, too, and I didn't go, didn't want to, all that way up, and all that bloody way down again, what a place for her to be in, better kipping anywhere that's handy. And saying it *again*, pulling at me, "Do come on up, Lena." Didn't. And I never spoke a single word, sort of couldn't find one to say. Well, God! I've been walking all that bloody way and look where I am.'

'It's the look in an eye that often gives you the answer.'

'What?'

'Keep away, keep clear. Don't want to know you.'

'Others do, you've met them. God, for instance. You remember that one.'

'Shall I laugh?'

'If you want to.'

'Listen.'

'I always did.'

'Listen now, he's talking, loves talking, christian name was George.'

'What is your name? Where do you live? How old are you? Who is your doctor? Like to know that, in case.'

'And have we your fingerprints?'

'Yes. And the footprints, too.'

'You're laughing in my ear.'

'You're only laughing in your own, dear.'

'Am I?'

'Get up. Go. Keep walking. *That's* the thing.'

'I'll do that.'

'Then *do* it.' In the end you might hear somebody laughing. It helps.'

She moved, paused at the kerb, looked down the road. 'Course. I know this place, you cross somewhere lower down,' crossed the road, stood, suddenly saw the lights. 'That's it. Used to cross here Wednesdays, remember now, way she used to hate those lights, used to pray there whilst she was waiting,' seeing further than the lights, a known corner, a byway, many a time walked, halting, moving again, getting lost amongst people, moving with them, reaching the other side, walking slowly into a known street, the shops coming clear, the sounds clearer. 'There it is,' the familiar door, the glass, the card hanging up, OPEN. Opening it, a bell ringing, a man at the counter, the same man, keeper of the secret, remembering a Wednesday morning smile.

'Good morning,' he said. 'Haven't seen you lately. I was told . . .'

'You heard?'

'Yes, and I am sorry about it,' leaning over the counter, looking at her, saying quietly, 'Funny thing, Mrs Biddulph but up to the very last day I wished there had been just one letter for your friend, just the one, from anywhere.'

'Made her happy, Mr Denton.'

'Yes, I suppose it did.'

'Morning.' Watching her go, the bell clanging, the door banged shut. Turning to his assistant, who knew everything, forgot nothing.

'She's Friday, Mr Denton.'

'Quite right. Her friend used to be Wednesdays.'

'She was rather funny, I thought.'

'Who was funny?'

'The other old lady that used to come in with her.'

'Yes, she used to have a special Wednesday morning smile, I expect you'll remember that, too, Fryer,' Mr Denton said.

'Seen them in The Marquis many a time,' Fryer said.

'Indeed! Would you mind continuing with the checking,' Mr Denton said, in a very official voice.

'Certainly, Mr Denton.'

'Good.'

*

She had wandered down the street from the Post Office, and now stood at the entrance to a large store. People hurried in and out, not noticing, even when they bumped into her.

'Such a nice man he was. And still there, same as ever.'

'You're blocking this doorway, madam.'

'Sorry.'

'Then move please, since you are still blocking it, madam.'

'Sorry.' Walking again, to the end of the street, turning, walking back again, staring in, seeing two heads close together.

'Saxby.'

'Yes, sir.'

'I'm sure I've seen that woman before. Watch her.'

'Yes, sir.'

A manager, musing.

'Something familiar about her, sure I've seen her somewhere before. But where?' and moving towards the window, staring at her, the long coat, the hat, no bag, 'That's it, never carried a handbag. Where the hell did I last see that woman?' Walking back again, and earnestly to Saxby. 'Seen her before?'

'Can't remember, sir.'

'Racking my bloody brains because I have seen her somewhere, something about her, look at her now, peering in, seen those looks before, God, you have to watch these days, you *really* have. It's the looking in, like they want something, like they intend to get it, a damned curse these days, the lifting that's going on. You haven't been here long enough yet, son, but you soon learn. Keep your eye open.'

'I shall, sir.' When he looked again she had gone. He walked to the door, looked up and down. Gone. 'She'll be back, they always come back. Wish to hell I could remember exactly what it is that's so familiar about the woman.' He checked his watch with the clock. A routine coming up.

'Saxby?'

'Yes, Mr Stevens?'

'Shan't be long.' He left the shop, again scanned the street, hurriedly crossed, went straight into The Marquis for his usual morning mild.

'Morning. Usual.' Sitting with it, and the only occupant of the pub, a loud hello to the licensee pushing aside a red curtain. 'Looks like rain.'

'Doesn't it just. You're slack,' Mr Stevens said. 'Mr Finch?'

'Yes?'

'There used to be two old women that sat in that corner, sometimes in the morning, but most often in the evening. Seen them many a time.'

'Wasn't one of them a tall thin woman?' Finch came to his table, sat down. 'Lots of women come in here,' he said, 'young and old. What rings a bell?'

'Well, there was a tall thin woman in a long coat and a black hat and she's just been staring hard through our window as though she simply loved the place. Blocked up the doorway for nearly five minutes, held up the traffic, told her to beat it. Funny, but I'm sure I've seen her somewhere. The other woman was tiny, compared.'

'Think I know who you mean. Little one jumped through a window the other day . . .'

'Oh!'

'You should read the papers,' Finch said. 'I think the woman you're curious about was named Biddulph, other one was named Kavanagh.'

'You may be right, Mr Finch. It was just this *something* bout her, ah . . .! I'll be off.'

'So long,' and as he reached the door, calling, 'Half a minute.' And Stevens thought, 'He's got the answer.'

'If you should see that woman, would you tell her there's a letter lying here for her.'

'Will do,' and the manager returned to the shop, unsatisfied, no clue. 'Pity.' Another look up and down, she wasn't there. 'She's gone.'

*

She walked through her days, remembered a park, went there, sat on a bench. No children, onc old man on a bench, kicking leaves.

'Yes, was here, forgotten which bench it was, nearly always the same one. No children at all today.' Looking at the man on the opposite bench, still kicking, hoping he wouldn't cross, she'd had that, 'so'd Brigid, too. Always find that lot in a park, peeping, watching.' Always close, and linking arms, walking to the end of streets, roads, no word spoken, knowing when they had had enough, knowing when they were tired, back to Gag Lane.

'Was nice there, cosy, nobody bothered you, and when you got sick of looking at the same things, you could go out again, for another walk. It was always the thing to do. Funny, really, way they used to cut your light off, nearly always on Tuesdays, come to think of it, like somebody in their office hated Tuesdays, and everything that went with it. Library then. Never knew such quiet, always warm there. Never read anything, never asked for anything, just sitting, nobody bothered you, fall asleep if you wanted to, like a big church in a way but no prayers, just the bent people over books, and the big clock that used to hang outside the gallery, 'spect it's still there. Some things never change.'

Still looking at the man, and suddenly a hand to her hat,

making it more secure, bending forwards, as if she was on the very point of getting up, walking straight down the leaf drowned path towards the gate.

'Way those old bastards stare at you.' And in a moment hating him, and cursing him, and rising, rushing at him, 'What the bloody hell are you staring at, you old . . .' and down the path, through the gate, on to the road. 'Christ! Another road. It's not far from here, but I don't think I'll go there, not today. Gag Lane, number five standing up straight, two others falling to pieces, not stood, but hanging, like draperies hang, nobody there, shifting them all out, that's it these days, "everybody out!" ' A nip in the air, and the light beginning to go, the promptings again.

'Why didn't you go? Said you were.'

'I did go, and then I came back again, and then I went on again, like I daren't stop walking, it was my feet, really, I didn't want to do a bloody thing 'cept sit down anywhere, and shut my eyes. My eyes are real tired. Just looking, feet hurt a bit, but not much. I'll be all right soon, know I'll be all right.'

'You have to *do* something.'

'That's what I'm thinking about, doing something. Will in a minute. You have to make up your mind about it first, and then you do it. Now you've got me back in that damned library and there I am looking at her, watching her all the time, dreading what I might hear any second, her snoring, she's like that, you know, tell soon's her head bobs. Sometimes she'd open her eyes, just look at you, warm, sometimes like she was telling you she was glad you were still there, sometimes as if you *wasn't*. Always knew what it meant then. *Tired*. Odd the way tiredness gets you at times. We were always glad to go then, had our little reverie, you might say, and she'd done her silent little think, that's the benefit, not the books, she never read a book in her whole life, I shouldn't think. I've read a few myself, once. I think it was only once she *really* snored, God, was I annoyed with her about it, ashamed, all those heads rising, turning and staring at us both, their eyes saying everything, glad it wasn't their lips. They hated being disturbed. Told us to go, so we went, kept by our motto, keep out of everybody's way, always the safest ticket to have in your hand. Yes indeed.' A sudden sigh. 'Where am I?'

'Still in the same place, I'm afraid, though you have done a lot of walking this morning. Perhaps you want to wear something out. Yes?'

'Perhaps.'

'You nearly walked into that store.'

'Know I did.'

'Not new.'

' 'Tis.'

'*Old.* Sold three months ago. Used to be a firm called Soonan's, one of those takeover larks. New staff, too, but the same manager's there. I expect you recognized him at once. You did stand there, staring through the window.'

'Two men there, one young, one old, younger one came at me right away, only on the step half a minute before he was at it. "Move off," he said, way he said it to me, real sharp he was. "You're blocking this *door*way, madam," and just before that somebody else came at me, woman it was, nearly knocked me on my back, she had a bag with her as big as a pillar box, you could put a bloody ship inside what she had. Didn't half let her have a look, sullen looking bitch she was, tell she'd been warm all night, looked it, could tell right away where *she* lived, but you always can, makes you feel like a bloody tramp.'

'And they're always about, a duty to do, really, they help each other to keep the rest of them out of the way, even out of *sight*, if they *could*, but fortunately this is still a free country, and they know it is.'

'Say it is.'

'Well it *is*. Free, real free.'

'Not arguing.'

'Then get bloody on then, 'stead of standing there, talking out anything comes into your head.'

'I *am* going.'

'Then God then, *go*. You've been saying that all the morning.'

'Have I?'

'Yes.'

'What the hell are you laughing at?'

'Just thinking if these roads were hills you'd have flattened them long since. Thought of that?' She hadn't, and she walked quickly down one side of the street, and slowly up the other, head down, feet aimless, road endless. The lights came on. She stopped, looked at the lights, the shop windows.

'Afternoon's over. Fancy. But I don't think I was walking *all* the while, and somebody said in my ear that I was. No lights Willesden way. Pity. Feel nothing without her now, nothing. Funny to think my thoughts floating all the way down the Thames, 'tis really,' a smile came and went, a mere flash. She walked on, having espied at the end of this street three large tea chests outside a shop that was closed, shuttered, in darkness. She sat down on one of these.

'My bloody feet.' Ache gone, weight gone. People passing by, people talking.

'Can't hear them, can't see.'

'Don't stay *too* long, you don't want those worn out words in your ears again.'

'Once, when I was little, a man came to our house and he said to my mother, "Is this her?" and she said, "Yes, that's her," and he said, "What a nice little girl," and my mother said, "Yes, isn't she?" and he said, "Let's hope she'll always be a nice little girl." Before a bell rang for school my mother insured me against fifteen different kinds of death.'

'Didn't know you had one.'

'Had. Just remember. Fancy remembering that, now, of *all* days, sitting on this bloody wooden box, three of them here, big strong boxes they are, too, and they're lying here as if nobody in the world ever owned them, or wanted to, like they'd just arrived here on one of them magic carpets, without a name and address.'

'Don't stay too long, you ought to know the rule, don't sit in any place *too* long, or the world will come along and have you fixed up final in the wink of an eyelid.'

'I am thinking about it, and I'm thinking about a lot of other things as well, and I'll tell you some of them.'

'Tell.'

'Keep your mouth shut, say nothing, I mean unless you have to, and never shout, and if you see some people coming round one corner, you go around another one quick. Course I always did that, we both knew, nothing at all on paper, knew it inside. Nobody could ever say that either of us ever got in anybody's way.'

'Somebody is watching you.'

'Can't see anybody.'

'You will soon, because it's the way things happen.'

'There's such singing going on in my feet, I mean from the relief of not having to stand on them too long, that I haven't a thought about seeing anybody. One or two nice things came into my head, I put glue on them so'd they stick, little *moments* that people have.'

'Don't *plan*.'

'Haven't.'

'*Sure?*'

'Daren't. Not now.'

'Grain of sense somewhere there. I'm glad, really. And I *mean* it.'

'I'll go any minute now.'

'Good. It's *always* good to know, at the right time, just what you want to do.'

'Yes.'

'Good. And if you do *do* that, then you'll fall asleep more easily, and the shape of the morning won't matter a single damn. Will it?'

'No.'

'Glad you know then.'

'Christ! What on earth are you trying to do? Teach me?'

'Don't expect a *message*.'

'Not expecting one.'

'There's one precious fragment still hanging on . . .'

'Don't tell me.'

'Somebody *else* is watching you now.'

'Let them.'

'You know there's no more roads?'

'Know.'

'No more letters, no more bells ringing at Mr Denton's pokey little Post Office.'

'Know.'

'No more bottles on the hob?'

'Yes.'

'Good.'

'I'd better get up, just go,' Mrs Biddulph said.

'Wait.'

'Well?'

'You have a habit, a *bad* habit, and a lot of people I know haven't forgotten it. And before you get up, go, leaving those lost tea chests behind you, and walking off on any road that's now of your own choice, remember to *strangle* that habit on the way.'

'I'll think about it.'

'The world's thinking about it, so you're in good company.'

'Thank you for that.'

'No thanks required.' She moved, rose stiffly off the tea chest, the feet protesting, taking the weight again.

'You know somebody is watching you. I told you twice already. You made no comment whatever. Incidentally the next road is *so* short you're at the end of it almost at once, as if it hadn't even had a beginning.'

'I know where I'm going,' Mrs Biddulph said.

'Be careful how you go, watch those that watch.'

'I always watch.'

'Good. Goodbye. Good luck, and no thanks necessary for that.' Walking again, not knowing, not thinking, not watching.

'Wait.'

'*Well?*'

'Somebody is watching you all the way.'

'I'll try to remember.'

'I'm glad. Goodbye again.'

'Good*bye*.' Walking again, up one side, and down the next, the lights drowning.

'Know this street,' Mrs Biddulph said. 'Know this place,' she said, stopped dead. Looked back, looked up, looked *in*.

*

'There she is again,' Stevens said, 'and Saxby, startled, said, 'Who?'

'That old bitch I told you about this morning. Christ, Saxby, in this business you have to be on your toes all the time, *all* the . . . time. Watch her.'

'Yes, sir,' Saxby said, and stood, and watched, and Mr Stevens gave a little run into his office and sat down, put his hands to his head, thought.

'Sure I'm right. I'm bloody certain I'm right.' Thought of The Marquis, Mr Finch. 'He was covering up, sure he was, yes, I'm damn sure he was covering up for that old bitch. Positive menace.' His hands made shaving movements over his forehead, his knuckles dug in, his mind diving, mining known territory, trying to remember. 'When? What bloody day was it, not long ago, I'm sure of it,' jumping to his feet, rushing out, calling, 'Saxby. Come *here*.' He came.

'She's still there, sir, looking in, never does anything else, just stood there, stiff, staring at me, *staring*.'

'Lot of them about these days, and mad bloody days they are, and don't I know it, once had a little shop on the corner myself, the old days, most hated thing in the world today, Saxby, the *old* days. Ah! Different then. Customer come in. Like a member of your own family, nice, no chatting now, Saxby, no time, get on, get bloody on, that's the crusade today, no waiting, every minute a knife.' Clutching his shoulder, giving him a little shake, 'Wake *up*, Saxby, know you're new here, not used to it, but by God, there's people going about today that would remove your eyeballs inside a split second.' A most dramatic pause, and then. 'She still watching?'

'Yes, sir.'

'Just carry on, lad,' Stevens said, 'rest's mine, my showery, the thing to be done, done, finishing off, letting the world know you're always on your damned toes.'

'Yes, sir. She's still looking in, like she's thinking of buying the whole shop.'

'Gets them like that,' Stevens said, 'but no known name for it, that is, in law.'

'No, sir.'

'Right.'

'Yes, sir.' A final nod to his sentinel, a quick turn round, a fugitive glance outwards, a quick turn again, and the words stabbing, 'What *is* her bloody name?'

Biddulph froze where she stood. When she looked left and right there were no roads. Something had come to an end.

'I'm sure I've been here before,' she said. 'Now what was the name again, what was . . . ?' The people there, slow and quick, purposeful, certain and not certain, the world's gorge placated here, under the lights that sometimes seemed too bright, too sure, the shelves towering, and what they held crying out for hands. The feast of eyes. The warmth of animate air and a forest of clutching hands, and Mrs Biddulph watched, and Mrs Biddulph waited. Her handmaid waited also, the total geography of calculation, of guile, the measure of fullness and emptiness, a total summation of the longest day, and the walking, and the wondering, and the throwing away, and more walking and more walking, this being a duty to do. The feet had the measure and the message. She never moved, but went on staring, and finally caught the eye that now began to stare her out, an echo in her ear. 'There is somebody watching.'

Stevens smiling, Stevens ogling, Stevens with all the expected responses of a never satisfied dog. Stevens who never forgot, and yet at this very moment was trying to remember, agonizing with it, staring and staring, searching for a name, an expression, a gesture, a particular movement with the cunning and the desperation that lay within it.

'Begins with a B. Sure it begins with a B. *What* is it?' If he waits long enough her hand will spell it out for him. And he went on watching. Another moment, an advancing lady in a fur coat, the coat that sang the song everywhere it went,

'I can buy *anything*.' A new absorption, the *other* technique, the voice in his ear.

'Smile. Smile big. Rub your hands, bow.' He smiled, he bowed.

'Now these, madam, these especially, yes, quite new altogether, a new idea in eating, yes, oh, you had heard of them. Well then. There!' The pot in her hand, and Stevens absorbed, and less aware of the shadow that had glided into the store, and Saxby bent to his knees, stroking the dog that was the final decoration in supermarketing.

'A nice little dog,' said Saxby.

'Isn't he just,' and a softer ha! ha! Mrs Biddulph stood where she had always stood. Looked right and left, listened, saw the small flask, put her hand on it, slipped it up her sleeve, advanced a few paces, slipped it down, into a capacious pocket. It was almost as though Mr Stevens had decided to close his darting eyes against the sudden sin. But Saxby *knew*, the knowledge of it as bright as a button. He walked up to the tall woman in the long black coat.

'Excuse me, madam.' Mrs Biddulph came to her full height. 'I never excuse anybody.'

'I saw you take a small bottle off the spirits shelf, madam.'

'I didn't.'

'I shall call the manager.'

'Call him,' Mrs Biddulph said, beginning to move, moving, her hand clenching a hidden bottle.

'Excuse me,' Saxby said. 'You cannot go, madam,' and held, and called 'Mr Stevens.'

Stevens flew, came abreast of her, cried, 'Ah! Got you. Yes *indeed*.' The world pressed in on all sides, watched, waited.

'This way,' and she went that way.

'Saxby.' Saxby understood.

'This *way*,' Stevens said, at last got the clutch that was right. The world spoke in half a dozen languages, looked at each other, as if to say, 'How exciting,' following, then as the office door closed, suddenly fragmenting, going about their business.

'Ring them?'

'Yes, Mr Stevens.'

'Good,' he said, and sat down. Mrs Biddulph stood, and he did not ask her to sit down, since now the message had been received, memory had rung the bell, and he spoke, abruptly, harshly.

'Watched you half the morning, your eagle eye on the window, madam, searched my mind for the last occasion, searching for names, just couldn't get yours,' and then a fulsome smile. 'Got it now.' And she said nothing.

'Biddulph,' he said, 'a Lena Biddulph. You used to go about with another lady, little one she was, used to think she might be your sister, so close you seemed to be. You understand the procedure, madam?' And Mrs Biddulph said nothing. Mr Stevens looked out of the window of his office, *wished* for the arrival that seemed to him so much delayed, at last saw her, a helmet approaching, and much liquid hair beneath, advancing on his office, rising, opening the door. 'This is her, constable.'

'Yes?' He put his hand into the Biddulph pocket, extracted a flask.

'Bold as you like, my assistant saw it, caught her, knew her as soon as he got her, been here before, yes indeed.'

'It's you then?' And Biddulph said nothing. Stevens glanced at the woman constable, his eye gave the message, 'We want to get on, the world's always on our back. We're very *busy*, constable.' She ignored the glance, said quietly, her hand already reaching out for a known arm.

'Mrs Biddulph, isn't it?' And Mrs Biddulph said nothing. Arm gripping arm, a slight pull. 'Come along,' the helmet said.

She came along.